DRAGON GAME

Reclaiming the Fire #3

Dragon Game

Reclaiming the Fire
Volume Three

Alicia Wolfe

For Missy.

Chapter 1

I smelled demon as soon as I passed through the door. The subtly acrid, bitter scent teased at my nose and sent a shiver of dread down my spine.

Suck it up, Jade, I told myself. After all, it wasn't like this was a surprise. I had just knowingly walked into a demonic lair. Was it too late to rethink my choice of career?

The receptionist brightened artificially. "May I help you, miss?"

A pretty young woman, she sat behind a plain metal desk. Behind her a bead curtain provided the only portal through a blank white wall into the chambers beyond. Even now there could be someone dying back there. The sign on the wall read MARA'S MASSAGES.

I put on my game face. "I'm Sally Jenson," I said, stepping to the desk. "Avon Regional Salesperson of the Month."

The receptionist's eyes jerked up and down my length, surely noting my conservative skirt and jacket with a slightly flashy blouse underneath, a metallic purple color that matched my pumps and the highlights in my wavy black hair.

"Good for you," she said. "But we're not buying."

I put on a condescending smile. "If you'll forgive me, I should talk to your manager or proprietor. Is Mara in?"

The receptionist's eyes narrowed. I sniffed, trying to decide if she was human or not. She didn't smell demonic, but I couldn't tell for sure. The demon smell permeating the air may have been masking something else.

"We don't deal with solicitors," she said.

I put on my best *let's-be-real* expression. In a less arrogant voice, I said, "I'll be honest, I know what this place is. And trust me, I have just the products the girls here need. I specialize in the unique requirements of ladies of the night. How do you think I got to be Regional Salesperson of the Month?"

"By selling makeup to whores?"

"It's a surprisingly booming market. *Someone* has to cater to it."

Sighing, she pushed a button on her desk phone. "Ma'am, there's a visitor here for you."

A moment passed, then a voice replied, "I'll send for her."

"You can wait over there," the receptionist told me, pointing to some empty chairs along the wall.

Before I could reach a seat, the door chimed and a man strode in—my partner Davril. That is, Lord Davril

Stormguard of the Fae Queen's Court, former king, current Fae Knight and all-around badass. His short, slightly curly blond hair flashed as his steel-blue eyes swept the room. He pretended not to notice me but went straight to the receptionist.

She watched him approach, a smile on her lips. He had dimmed his inner light and wore his street clothes—jeans, a tight blue T-shirt under a brown leather jacket. His T-shirt stretched across his abs as he walked.

"I'd like a date," he said.

"A hunk like you doesn't need to pay for it."

"I don't like to waste my time. I like to get right down to business."

If only that were true, I thought.

The receptionist named a dollar figure, he agreed, and she showed him into the backroom. When she returned, I pretended to browse through the collection of skin magazines. Shortly a young woman in a red sequined dress slit high up the side emerged from the bead curtain and approached me.

"You wish to see the madam?"

"Absolutely!" I sprang to my feet, clutching my briefcase of supposed samples.

"You'll have to leave that here, I'm afraid. Madam won't allow any briefcases in the back."

I nodded and placed the case on a chair. There went most of my weapons.

"This way," said the woman, or whatever she was. The whole place stank of demon, but the odor seemed stronger near her. She might look like a human, but she was probably something else. It was with grave misgivings that I followed her through the curtain and into the back.

Grunts and gasps surrounded me, coming through thin walls, and the smell of sex hit me like a shovel. My pulse spiked, and it suddenly grew hot. Was Davril already in a room? Just how was he going to deal with his, er, masseuse?

We hadn't gone over *that* particular bit of the plan, I realized belatedly. *You'd better not get too far into your role, Dav.*

"In here," said the woman in the red dress, ushering me into a small office with cheap walls and a cheaper desk. This whole place was just as rundown and mediocre as I'd known it would be after having staked it out for two weeks. Still, I couldn't help but feel that a den of deadly succubi, a place of sex and murder and the demonic, should be a bit more, well, atmospheric.

The madam sprawled behind her desk in an armchair, the only thing vaguely luxurious about this whole place. I recognized her immediately—petite, black-haired, with lively blue eyes and a pouty red mouth. She wore a black mini-dress with black sequins to go with her hair.

"Avon calling?" she purred.

I wanted to punch her in that pouty mouth. Just how many men's souls had she slurped down past those lips?

"That's right," I said brightly. "I specialize in just your trade. In fact, I—"

A horrible scream sounded to my right, coming through the thin walls. I froze, my heart almost stopping. For a moment I thought the voice was Davril's, but no, he'd been a few rooms down, and his voice was deeper. But still, I knew what that scream must mean. A man was getting his soul ripped out.

I spun to the door.

The woman in the red dress had come in after me, and she blocked it off. I socked her in the jaw. I'm half shifter, even if I can no longer shift, and I'm stronger and faster than a normal human.

She, however, was a demon. She rebounded immediately and launched herself at me. Her arms stretched out and her hands transformed into talons. Her face elongated, and her mouth bristled with awful fangs.

I stumbled backward. My butt hit the desk.

The madam's hands, now talons too, clamped my arms to my side.

The succubus in red flew at me, shrieking hideously. Dredging up the training I'd been receiving over the last few months, I waited for her to come close, then opened my legs, snapped them closed around her, seizing her around the middle. With a grunt, I threw her to the side, and she smashed into a wall.

The movement and the weight dislodged me from the madam's grip. I sprang to my feet and whirled to face her. From a nearby room came grunts and Fae swears. Davril must be battling the demon that had been about to give him a massage.

"Bitch!" the madam said to me. Her eyes glowed red, and spittle sprayed past her fangs. She's been petite and pretty a few seconds ago, but those had been a long few seconds. I mean, sheesh. Veins bulged in her face, and she stank of sulfur.

"Thought you could trap me?" I said, coiling myself for battle. I wished I'd been able to bring my weapons in.

"I don't know what you're talking about," she said.

Interesting. That must mean the scream I'd heard was unplanned. A succubus had just gotten carried away, right when I'd been about to give my sales pitch. Oh well. Saved me the trouble. I wasn't much of a salesperson, anyway.

"Who are you?" the madam hissed.

"I'm a Fae Knight, and you're under arrest on the order of the Queen." I relished the words. They were the first time I'd ever said them aloud. On the other hand, it felt really weird to be *arresting* someone. Me, a semi-reformed cat burglar.

Mara, if that was her name, sneered. "You're no Fae."

Banging noises erupted to my right. Davril must have dealt with the succubus he'd been given and now he was moving against the one who had killed or tried to kill the man who'd screamed. Maybe the man could be saved. He was a pig, sure, but he didn't deserve to die because of it.

"It's honorary," I said, and started to jump across the room at the madam.

The succubus in the red dress had recovered, though. She latched onto my ankle. I growled and kicked her in the face. She slumped back. By then the madam was already descending on me, talons outstretched to wrap around my throat. Her body met mine and toppled me to the floor. I punched her in the ribs, then the face. Her talons wrapped around my throat and squeezed.

"I would drink your soul," she said. "But I only do men. Sorry, hon."

I tried for a witty comeback but couldn't speak. I couldn't breathe either. I bucked against her, striking her repeatedly, but she wouldn't budge. Stars spun around her. Lights flickered, then began to dim. I was about to pass out.

At the last instant, I remembered my training.

With all my remaining strength, I cupped my palms slightly, then smashed them against her ears, breaking her eardrums. She screamed and jerked up, her talons leaving my neck. Blood gushed from her ears. I gasped for air.

Before I could subdue her, the door crashed open. Davril, breathing hard, his blond hair sweaty and in disarray, stalked in with murder in his eyes.

"Jade, are you okay?"

I nodded, wheezing.

He helped me off the floor. "Don't worry, your first time never goes the way you plan."

We turned to the madam. She glared at us both, her hands holding her ears. Blood trickled through her fingers.

"You, madam, are under arrest," said Davril.

"That was my line," I croaked. I needed a lozenge.

The plan had been for us to come in quietly, infiltrate the demons' camp and then subdue them individually in private rooms. The madam, however, seemed to have other ideas.

"Fuck off," she said.

She hissed, spraying acidic spittle that sizzled on the carpet, and shifted into her demon form. Black bat-like wings sprouted from her back, shredding her dress, and curling horns burst out from her forehead. Her feet morphed into black hooves. Her skin shimmered into mottled red.

Davril whipped out a pair of gleaming cuffs and advanced on her. "You can come peacefully or you can come otherwise—your choice. But you're not leaving here free to prey on innocent men again."

"They weren't so innocent," she said, and launched a hoof at his face.

He dodged aside, sweat flying.

I sprang forward, meaning to tackle her, but one of her claws swiped at my eyes. I ducked, breathless, and was forced to retreat. She was faster now that she'd stopped pretending to be human.

Growling, she aimed one of her palms at the ceiling. Crackling red energy built on the palm, then flashed upward, blasting a hole in the ceiling. Dust and plaster rained down, but she ignored the debris. Davril stretched out his own palm, and white light gathered there, then flared out toward the madam. Her free hand absorbed the blast, gathered its energy, then directed it back toward him. He dove to the floor. The energy passed through the air where he'd just been.

She laughed, pumped her wings and flew toward the gap she'd created in the ceiling.

"I don't think so," I said.

With my shifter reflexes, I jumped and grabbed onto one of her hooves. Her wings pumped harder, but I was too heavy.

"Bitch!" she said.

She kicked me in the side of the head with her other hoof. I lost hold and fell to the floor. Thankfully my instincts kicked in (har har) and I landed nimbly. Davril was just getting to his feet beside me.

"Later, assholes!" the madam said.

She vanished through the hole. Through it I could see that her escape wouldn't be that easy. A dozen Fae Knights on pegasuses, led by none other than the captain of the Order of the Shield himself, Lord Julus Gleamstone, drove toward her in a wedge. We'd hoped to end this without a big show of force, but we'd come prepared just in case. Magical nets spun through the air toward her, hurled by the knights in their gleaming armor.

She blasted more crimson lightning out of her palms, and the nets burned to a crisp. She shot her deadly energy toward the knights coming at her. Frustrated, they divided around her like water around a boulder. She flew higher.

"She's getting away!" Davril said.

"Not so fast," I said.

I whistled. Seconds later my flying motorcycle, its black raven wings pumping gracefully, sailed through the hole in the ceiling and alit on the ground before me. Smiling smugly, I jumped astride it.

"Want to climb on the back?" I asked Davril.

"I've got my own ride."

I knew he hadn't whistled for it himself because he didn't want Lady Kay to tear down half the building. Nice, right? Well, I'd show him that nice cops didn't catch evil demons.

Grinning, I gunned the motor and shot the motorcycle upward through the hole. Above me, Mara was vanishing into the clouds. The pegasuses pursued her, their white wings almost seeming to glow, but she threw one red blast at them after another. I patted the crossbow in its sheath mounted to the side of the bike, then drew it out and checked that a bolt was loaded. The bike wobbled, but I gripped it firmer by the handle with my left hand, stabilizing it. I'd have to learn how to ride and shoot at the same time someday. *Might as well be today.*

Above me, Mara turned around and fired a blast in my direction. I swerved around it. She fired another. I dodged this one, too. Brought up my crossbow and centered it on her back. Just as she turned to fire another blast, I squeezed the trigger. The bolt, lathered with a sleeping potion, struck her under the left shoulder blade, right where the left wing sprouted.

She stiffened, and the magical glow that had been building on her palm faded.

"Got you," I said.

She paused in mid-air. Slowly, her wings stopped flapping. She fixed me with a glare of purest hate, then her eyes clouded over and she fell from the sky, totally unconscious.

"Shit," I said, as she plummeted right past me.

Below, several pegasi tried to catch her, but she was falling right by them. *Damn.* She would hit the ground and never face judgment for her crimes. Fae Knights weren't assassins, they were cops. We brought people in, not killed them.

Grinding my teeth, I turned the bike around and aimed for the succubus. I knew I was too late, though. She was already dwindling to a speck below. In moments she'd crash right through the roof of the New Jersey strip center she'd just vacated.

Sunlight flashed on silver chrome. White wings stretched to either side of a gleaming 1960s-style muscle car, and I whooped. Davril, driving his auto-steed Lady Kay, was swooping in right under Mara. Even as he pulled under her, the top cycled down, Lady Kay becoming a convertible. Davril dipped the backseat, cushioning the blow just as Mara smacked right into it.

I joined the pegasi led by Lord Gleamstone, and we streamed by Davril to ensure that Mara was safely secured. She was.

As I passed by him, Davril turned to me, and we exchanged a hot smile. The action had really gotten both of our bloods going. Seeing that look on his face, my heart skipped a beat, and something fluttered in my belly.

Then I was past, but the feeling remained.

Uh oh.

Chapter 2

"Great work," said Lord Gleamstone, striding back and forth before us.

Davril and I stood before the massage parlor while the other Fae Knights brought out the limp bodies of four succubi, plus two unconscious johns—still alive, I was glad to see, and with their souls intact. The one that had screamed earlier had only been in the beginning process of having his essence ripped out, and he was going to make it. The other had been struck over the head by his "masseuse" when the violence had broken out and was starting to come around. I wondered how the johns would explain things to their wives (if they had them) when they got back home. Well, that was their lookout.

"You apprehended the hellspawn without any loss of life, whether on our side or theirs," continued Lord Gleamstone to Davril and me.

I swallowed, my throat still store. "It could have gone a little smoother."

"You did fine," Davril said, and I thrilled at the warmth in his voice—and the heat. Davril still looked like his blood was still raging. I was glad to see it, since mine was. I wanted to drag him into one of the massage rooms and have my way with him as soon as the Commander finished speaking, and I couldn't help but wonder if Davril would let me.

Lord Gleamstone seemed to sense something of what was going on between us, but he ignored it. "Before you start on the paperwork and enjoy some, er, downtime, the Queen wants to speak with you two."

"Both of us?" I said. That was interesting.

"She sent word just before the fighting started. You were already in position, so I had to wait until afterward to tell you. But yes, she wants a word with you both at your earliest convenience."

Davril's brows drew together. "Did she say what it was about?"

"No, only that it had something to do with …"

"Yes?"

Gleamstone cleared his throat. "With your brother."

Davril grimaced. I knew the subject of his brother Nevos was a sore one, and for good reason. Before Nevos betrayed him and sided with the Shadow, Davril had been a king and the Fae Lands had been at peace. Now the Fae Lords were in exile on Earth and the Shadow was triumphant in their homeworld.

Nevos, however, was now in *our* world. We'd been looking for some sign of him for two months.

"Has there been a sighting?" I asked Gleamstone.

"'Has there been a sighting, *sir*?'" he corrected me.

I mentally kicked myself. I was still getting used to all these rules and niceties. In the criminal underworld I was familiar with, we didn't use "sir" and "ma'am" very often.

"Sir," I said.

"Again, I know only what I told you. Now I suggest you visit Queen Calista immediately."

Lord Gleamstone moved off to oversee the transportation of the succubi. Already they were being placed in a metal cage drawn by six pegasi. They would be taken to the Adjudicator of the Realms and, if found guilty of being on this plane illegally, or of violating the rules of this plane, they would be sent back to hell. Good riddance, I thought.

Madam Mara hissed and sputtered from inside the black cage, but she did it weakly. She was still pretty dopey.

A crowd was forming. Already a few reporters snapped pictures or spoke before rolling cameras. I made sure to keep my face lowered. The last thing I needed was for any of my old cronies to see me working with the Fae Lords on live TV.

"We really need to get me a disguise or something," I said.

"We will," Davril said. "Next time we go out I'll give you a glamour. It will mask your real identity, just in case."

"Like, I'll have someone else's face?"

"Exactly."

I tapped my chin. "Anyone's? I mean, I could be Jennifer Lopez?"

"That's a celebrity? I would advise against it."

I batted my eyelashes at him. "Who would you *like* me to look like?"

"Oh, I don't know. Perhaps ... your sister?"

I punched his arm. "Bastard!"

He laughed, and I felt heat spread through me. Laughing a little, too, I said, "Well, I'll think about it. I guess it should really just be a random face. I'd like it to be a not-bad one, though."

The humor drained away from him as he scanned the horizon. He must be thinking about Nevos. Talk about a mood killer.

He gestured to Lady Kay. "Shall we?"

He'd attached a rack on the back just for my motorcycle, and together we strapped my ride to his, then climbed into Lady Kay, him behind the wheel and me in the passenger seat. He hit the gas and we shot up into the sky, leaving New Jersey behind. We were bound for Manhattan and the Palace of Lady Calista, queen of the Fae-in-exile. Wind whipped my hair out behind me and I had to fight the urge not to throw my feet up on the dash. Davril hated that. The sun warmed my skin, and I was still flushed from battle.

Out of the corner of my eye, I could see Davril being all broody and frowny. I wished I could find some way to bring us back to that flirty, randy place we'd just been. We both loved action, and it always got us going. Sooner or later I kept hoping it would get us all the way. And if it hadn't been for Commander Gleamstone's mention of Nevos, I felt we might have gotten there today. Damn it all.

"That was some fight," I said, trying to lighten the mood.

Davril just grunted. "Yeah."

"That madam almost had me there for a moment. Thanks for the rescue, by the way."

"Yeah."

"I hate to be the maiden in distress, but I do love a knight in shining armor."

"Yeah." He cleared his throat. "Excuse me?"

I sighed. "Nothing."

Soon we entered Manhattan, and its brilliant skyscrapers surrounded us. The castles of the Fae Lords topped many of them, with gorgeous towers and walls, intricate statues and fountains spurting from their courtyards. Some were light and airy, some were harsh and intimidating, but the largest and most beautiful of them all was the Palace, which erupted from the tallest skyscraper in New York. White and dazzling, its towers and walls shone with an inner radiance. We made straight for it.

As always, it was a hive of activity, with Fae coming and going on pegasi or other steeds. A human delegation was just leaving from one of the towers on a dirigible, and when I pointed it out to Davril he said, "Yes. Queen Calista regularly meets with politicians and officials of your world. That could be the Governor or perhaps the chief of police. The President even visits occasionally."

"I'd love to be a fly on *that* wall. Well, if flies weren't gross and disgusting. Maybe a butterfly? Someone really needs to change that expression."

Davril brought Lady Kay into the hangar that the Fae Knights used, and we each saw to our separate steeds, washed and dressed in our uniforms, then met back up. As we made our way through the halls of the Palace toward the Throne Room, I said, "Wonder why she wants to meet with *both* of us?"

"It's not your first time to meet with Her Highness."

"I know, it's just that … well, it's your brother. I know all things related to him are considered top secret."

"Jade, you underestimate yourself. You've proven worthy in the past, so why not now?"

"Maybe. But I think something's up."

"Up?"

I shrugged. "I guess we'll find out soon enough."

Lord Greenleaf met us at an intersection. Tall and severe, he was the Grand Vizier. Frosty as a winter ocean, he'd never taken a liking to me, but he seemed competent and loyal enough.

"I'm to take you to Her Majesty," he said, and led the way deeper into the Palace.

We passed a wall made of waterfalls, then passed down a corridor seemingly fashioned completely of exotic blossoms that gave off heady and intoxicating scents. The whole thing was baked in Fae magic, and it only grew stronger as we neared the Throne Room. I was pleasantly unsteady on my feet. I'd been here many times before, of course, but I never *quite* got used to it.

That was a good thing, though. It meant I never took it for granted. If I ever did, that would be a sad day indeed.

"So anything you can tell us?" I asked Greenleaf.

"Regarding?"

"The meeting," I said, as though it were obvious. It probably was, too. But Greenleaf was catty that way.

"I have nothing to impart," he said loftily.

I rolled my eyes at Davril. He pretended to ignore me.

Greenleaf led us past the royal guards and into the massive Throne Room with its crystal dome overhead and virtual forest below. Sunlight shone down through the crystal onto the beautiful trees and exotic animals that darted among them. The forest had completely grown back after the troll attack several months ago, but the devastation was still fresh in my mind. Mistress Angela had killed many of the Fae that day. She'd nearly killed the Queen, too.

Greenleaf ushered us through the forest and up the grand crystal stairs to the crystal throne high above. Queen Calista was just finishing up speaking with a group of nobles. Seeing us, she said her goodbyes to them, and they bowed and left.

"My lady, may I present Lord Stormguard and Lady Jade?" Greenleaf said.

"Shouldn't it be Lord Davril and Lady Jade?" I said. "Or Lord Stormguard and Lady McClaren?"

Greenleaf frowned at me.

"What?" I said. "I mean, that makes sense, right? If you're going by last names with the whole lord and lady thing, then do that. Or use first names. But different treatment just because I'm a woman isn't cool."

"Is this really necessary?" Davril muttered.

"I'm inclined to agree," Queen Calista said.

Greenleaf visibly repressed a rebuke at me. "Very well, Jade McClaren," he said. "Do you want me to refer to you as Lady McClaren?"

"Hell no," I said. "I love being called Lady Jade!"

He narrowed his eyes at me. I resisted the urge to stick my tongue out at him. I loved nettling him. It was so easy.

It was the Queen's turn to sigh. "Can we move this along, please? Lord Greenleaf, I would like to speak with these two alone."

The Grand Vizier bowed and withdrew. Davril and I turned to the Queen.

"I heard about your raid on the succubus nest," Her Majesty said. "That was well done."

"Thank you, Your Grace," Davril said.

"It's all in the wrist," I said.

"I'm sure." Calista studied Davril. In a more gentle, personal tone of voice, she said, "Your brother has been spotted."

Davril's face didn't betray any emotion. "May I ask where?"

"The Guild of Thieves."

His brows drew together. "What would he want with them?"

"I can't imagine." The Queen shifted her attention to me. "Jade, what do you know of the Thieves Guild?"

"Well, they tried to recruit me a few years ago," I said.

"You said no?"

I nodded. "They were small-time then, and they demanded a cut of any job I'd pull in exchange for membership."

"What would you have gotten out of it?" Davril said.

"Contacts, mainly. People to hook up with who were looking to plan a heist. You know, sometimes there's someone who has a way into a certain place, but he needs muscle, or a codebreaker, or a witch, or whatever. So the Guild is kind of like a dating service for thieves."

"Evidently you didn't require their services," the Queen said.

"Ruby and I were already getting referrals by then. We didn't need them. Also …" I grimaced, suddenly uncomfortable.

"Yes?"

I debated with myself, then said, "They wanted Ruby."

"Excuse me?" Davril said.

"They said that since we were partners I couldn't join without Ruby also joining, because then she'd be receiving the benefits of joining without the cost. They wouldn't allow that, and I didn't want to drag Rubes deeper into my pit, so I said no. Like I said, we didn't need them. Lately, though …"

Queen Calista leaned forward. "Yes?"

"Well, they've been getting more powerful. More aggressive. More and more of the underworld are in league with them. I guess it shouldn't be a surprise that Nevos would seek them out. I mean, Angela's hip deep in the underworld, and Nevos is in with her, so why not?"

Davril regarded me, then the Queen. "Your Grace, is this why you requested Jade's presence?"

Calista was silent a long moment. "Yes, I wanted her insight on the Guild, but … there's something more."

I felt a shudder work down my spine. "More?"

One of her hands reached out to grab the armrest of her throne. "Jade, you know I only want good things for you. I want you to be safe, and I would never put you in harm's way if I could avoid it."

The *but* in that sentence was about a mile wide.

"But?" I said.

"Lord Nevos has indeed made contact with the Thieves Guild, and he seems to be spending some time there. For what purpose, we don't know. But we do know that Angela's failsafe plan, after failing to kill me, was to liberate Nevos from that mirror so that he could lead his army to destroy us."

"The army's toast," I said.

"Yes, and thank you both for that," Calista said graciously. "Unfortunately, Nevos is not. And he is a high servant of our arch-foe, Lord Vorkoth."

Davril's hands bunched into fists at his side, then unclenched. "I've told her the story, my lady."

"Then you understand how deadly Nevos is, Jade. He's the one who literally opened the door for the Shadow before."

That cold shudder was starting to spread throughout my body. "You're afraid he's going to open another door."

Again, she nodded. "The final one, this time. There's nowhere else for us to run. And if the Shadow comes for us here …"

"The whole earth will suffer," I finished.

"Exactly."

Davril watched her, then me, then the Queen again. "Your Grace, are you saying what I think you are?"

Calista's vibrant green eyes fixed on me. "Lady Jade … my friend … I will not give you this order. I know how dangerous it will be. This will be a volunteer mission only."

I groaned inwardly. As if I could really refuse after all that. What was more, she was right.

"I know you've given up thieving," Calista went on, and I tried not to grimace. The truth was I hadn't, not exactly. But she didn't know that. "I'm asking you to take up the mantle again, however, or at least to pretend to show some interest in it."

"You want me to infiltrate them, don't you? The Thieves Guild?"

"Yes, Jade. I want you to join them, and through them find out what Nevos and Angela are up to. And stop them."

*   *   *

Gorgeous pink blooms sprouted from the thick vines that grew along the white walls, filling the hallway with the smells of citrus and lavender, but I barely noticed. My mind churned, and so did my guts. Davril strode at my side, lost in his own thoughts. Doubtless he was imaging coming to grips with his brother.

"She doesn't ask for small favors, does she?" I said, trying to make light of it.

"No. She doesn't." He seemed to shake himself out of his funk. "But you didn't have to say yes."

"You know I did. Shit, it's the right thing to do. What else could I have said?"

"You responded as a Fae Knight, Jade. I'm proud of you."

We entered the Tower of the Shield, where the knights were quartered. Normally I might ascend to the records room and resume going through the Fae archives in order to find my own nemesis, Vincent Walsh, the man who'd stolen my fire and killed my father and grandmother. But today I was in no mood to concentrate on that. My revenge could wait, at least a little.

Davril walked with me to the door of my room. I opened it and passed inside, then turned on the threshold to face him. We stared at each other. A few knights passed in the hall, but our eyes didn't waver from each other. The knights disappeared. Davril stayed where he was. My heart beat against my ribs in a staccato rhythm. *Bu-DUMP bu-DUMP*.

"Davril," I managed.

"Jade."

That heat I'd felt during the battle returned. His face was tense, but his eyes burned, and I swear I could see a pearl of sweat beginning to bead on his forehead.

"I'm sorry you had to lie," I said.

He cleared his throat. "Pardon?"

"I mean, about my thieving." He was the only Fae that knew I was still a cat burglar when I wasn't policing the infractions of the city's supernatural criminals. Having to keep that secret vexed him, I knew, but for me he was willing to do it—and also because it made me better at what I did.

He gently pushed me forward, coming into my apartment, then closed the door behind him.

"We shouldn't talk about that in public," he said.

"Right. Sorry."

But not *that* sorry. We were all alone in my little set of rooms, and my blood buzzed with adrenaline.

For a long moment, we just stood there, about an inch apart, staring at each other.

"I should go," he said. But he didn't move.

"Uh-huh," I said.

Slowly, hardly daring to believe my own courage, I reached out and grabbed his hand. *Jade, what the hell are you doing?* part of my mind screamed. *Why did you wait so long?* screamed another.

"Jade," Davril said. "I'm not sure …"

"I'm not either."

My skin was hot. As if in a dream, he took his arm and wrapped it around my waist. His firm hand pressed into the small of my back, bringing me in closer to him. Gulp.

I tilted my face up toward him.

He bent his head down. His lips came toward mine. Right as they began to touch, brushing mine briefly, so that I could feel the warmth of his skin, he wrenched himself backward.

"No," he said, his voice coarse.

My cheeks burned. "I'm sorry. I-it was a mistake."

"It … wasn't a mistake, Jade."

My pulse spiked. "No?"

His square-jawed head swung back and forth. "No."

I swallowed. I couldn't speak.

"But it can never happen," he added.

I reached out toward him, but he turned away. In moments he was out the door. It closed softly behind him, and I stared at it, my heart pounding wildly. Tears welled behind my eyes, but I wouldn't let them out. Frustration mounted in me. We'd come so close! Why had he stopped? Was there something wrong with me? Was it because I was a criminal? Because I'd made him break his vows? *Damn!*

I sucked in a great big breath. It was probably for the best, I told myself. That's why he'd stopped. It would have made things too complicated. We were partners, and that's all we could be.

Right?

But *It can never happen?* That sounded monstrously dire. That sounded like he was closing a door, and I couldn't accept that.

I swore, took a cold shower and had dinner by myself. When I could concentrate, I climbed the tower and pored over the records for a few hours. Still no sign of Walsh. *You can't hide from me forever, you bastard.* After I'd exhausted myself, I went to bed, but sleep proved difficult. I knew that tomorrow I would have to infiltrate the Thieves Guild. And seek out Nevos.

So why did I keep dreaming about Davril?

It was only in the morning that I realized something that I'd missed, or that I hadn't allowed myself to think about. The Thieves Guild had demanded that Ruby and I join up together last time. They wouldn't take me without her. Did they still have the same policy? I cycled through the numbers on my phone, finding the recruiter that had contacted me back then, and dialed him. The connection failed, as it often did inside the Palace—something to do with magic and modern technology not always jiving—so I went out onto a balcony and tried again. That worked.

"Yeah, you'll both have to sign up together," said Mailon, the recruiter, after I'd posed my question. "I mean, if you're still working together, that is."

"Well, we work together *sometimes*," I said. Maybe there was still a way I could keep Ruby out of this.

Mailon chuckled. "Don't lie to me, Jade. In the Guild, we don't fool around. If you tell us you don't work with her and sign up alone, then later we find out you lied, you know what happens."

I knew. The Guild was developing a fairly sinister reputation lately, and part of that came from things like this. They didn't tolerate disrespect or lies—kind of funny coming from an organization composed entirely of criminals.

"Death," I said.

"That's right, Jade. So tell me true: are you still working with Ruby?"

Chapter 3

"Okay."

"*Okay?*" I said. That wasn't what I'd expected to hear. But Ruby just stared back at me with an almost bored expression on her face. "Are you sure you understood me?"

She stuck her tongue at me. "You said you wanted me to join the Guild of Thieves with you."

"I *don't* want you to. I want you *not* to."

"But you're still asking me."

I tried not to grind my teeth. She was so infuriating. We stood in the kitchen of the apartment we shared—that is, whenever I wasn't at the Palace—and she was trying to get the cork off a wine bottle without ruining her nails. They were red to go with her hair.

"I know you wouldn't ask if it weren't important," she added. The cork popped off, and she poured herself a glass of red, then one for me.

I hesitated a moment, then downed a sip. "Wow, that's tart," I said.

"Bitch bitch bitch," she laughed.

I stared at her over the brim. "This is no joking matter, sis. The Guild of Thieves is dangerous."

"I *know*. Grrr, I'm not a *baby*." She paused, the glass halfway to her lips. "Where did they come from, anyway? No other city has a guild like that, right?"

I rolled my shoulders. "It started after the Fae Lords came, and all the shifters and mages and such came out of the shadows. Magic totally changed the criminal underworld. Some people thought we needed to start getting organized. We needed people who had a way in to a secure location to be able to find people who knew how to disable the magical booby-traps there. That kind of thing. The guild was small time at first, but now they're flexing their muscle."

"And they're kind of dicks."

"If by dicks you mean evil, then yeah, kind of." I took another sip, then set the glass down. I needed to be relatively sober for what I wanted us to attempt. I wanted her sober, too. "You'd better quit or we won't be able to go tonight."

"You want to go … right now?"

"There's no reason to delay. Already Nevos could be getting what he wants."

She slurped her wine, then made a face at me. "Party pooper."

"Actually, I hear the Guild of Thieves throws some pretty righteous shindigs."

Her eyebrows shot up. "Yeah?"

"Yeah."

She beamed. "Then what are we waiting for?" She downed the rest of her wine, burped, then stoppered the bottle.

I cleared my throat. She fixed me with a look.

"This isn't a social thing," I said. "They'll probably want to give us some sort of test or something. It could even be dangerous. And if they let us in, we'll be bound by their rules and codes of secrecy. And they take that stuff seriously."

"I got, I got it. Sheesh! Now can we go before I rethink this whole thing?"

Part of me had really been hoping that she'd wimp out and not want to do it. As her sister, I couldn't stand the idea of putting her in jeopardy. But I knew this was the right thing to do. Nevos meant to bring the Shadow to our world, and for some reason he wanted the help of the Guild of Thieves to do it. I needed to know what they knew. Maybe even get access to the traitorous Fae Lord himself.

What would happen if I did? Could I kill him? I wasn't sure if I could just murder someone like that, and anyway that should be Davril's thing, not mine. But either way I might be able to get close to him, find out what he was up to and stop him.

"Well, sis?" Ruby said. "Are we going or not? My buzz is wearing off."

I'd parked on the roof, casting an invisibility spell over my sweet, sweet bike, so we marched upstairs and decloaked it. Gorgeous raven-black wings spread out from all that black metal and chrome, poised dramatically.

Ruby whistled. "You do have a bitchin' ride, girl."

I stroked the handlebars. "Don't I know it. Come on, get on."

We were taking my motorcycle because we could both fit on it and bring Ruby's broom, too. She strapped it to her back on a little sling she'd attached to it, then flung her arms around my waist as I goosed the throttle and shot us off into the sky. She whooped as we climbed higher. The motorcycle's black wings stretched out to either side, stroking the air with powerful pumps, and the engine throbbed between my thighs. Below us lights of nighttime New York glimmered like stars. Cold wind ripped at us, flinging my hair and making my eyes mist.

"Let me," Ruby said, and muttered a quick spell. Instantly the wind died and it grew warmer.

"Thanks," I said. I knew some magic, too, but Ruby was the true witch, and she was much more adept at it than I ever could be.

I drove us to a seedy area of downtown, then landed on the road and kept driving. My ride tucked her wings up as I coasted along the street. Some pedestrians turned to watch appreciatively, but in post-Fae-rival New York aerial vehicles weren't that uncommon, and they quickly went about their business.

"There," I said, pointing to a Gothic-looking building composed of dark brick, with large, ornate windows and gargoyles perched on the ledges. There weren't any free parking spaces, so Ruby and I climbed off the bike. It stretched out its wings again and flew upwards. It would circle until I whistled for it, then it would come to collect us.

"I bet that saves a lot on parking," Ruby said.

"You bet."

"Have you named her yet?"

I sighed as the motorcycle vanished around the side of a building and was momentarily lost to view. "No. And it might not be a she."

"Yeah?"

I shrugged. "I mean, Davril's ride is female, so why can't mine be male?"

"True, I guess. So it's male?"

"No. It's female."

She stuck her tongue out at me. "Lame-o. Anyway, so no name?"

"I can't think of one. I started to call her Bike-a-rella, but …"

"But it sucks?"

"Pretty much."

We regarded the looming, Gothic presence of the Guild House. Its gargoyles glared down at us with sinister expressions. Its grand door was truly huge, and its knocker was a big brass lion's head.

"Could they *get* any more cliché?" Ruby said.

"Yeah, they're really going for a certain look, aren't they? Gotta admit, I like the gargoyles, though. Nice touch."

"I just hope these ones don't fly."

I grimaced. "Don't give them any ideas."

We approached the steps, then climbed them. An aura of quiet mystery surrounded the building, which looked to be about ten stories, and I'm sure it was an atmosphere the Guild cultivated. They didn't exactly want tourists knocking on the door, right?

Speaking of which …

I grabbed the big brass knocker and banged on the door. Hollow booms reverberated within, and Ruby and I traded uneasy glances.

"I'm starting to get a bad feeling about this," she said.

"Bah. I'm sure this is all for show. It's probably an endless Cinco de Mayo in there."

"It better."

I squeezed her hand. "It's not too late to back out, sis. I can join alone."

"But then we couldn't do any more jobs together, right?"

"Well, not on pain of death, no. We wouldn't let a little thing like that stop us."

She rolled her eyes and groaned. "Fine, let's just do this. Why are they taking so long to answer the door?"

As if in response, the huge doors swung open, revealing a huge chamber wreathed in shadow with a stairway leading up into rooms on the far side. Feeling something cold curdle in my gut, I stepped across the threshold. *Here goes nothing.* Ruby swore under her breath and followed me. Together we stood in a grand lobby with marble floors and gleaming brass railings on the walls and staircase. Brooding oil portraits hung on the walls. The air was cool but dry.

Not a single person could be seen.

I stomped one of my sensible heels, and an echo rang throughout the lobby, off the marble floors and throughout the halls beyond.

"Hello?" I called. "Hell-ooo?"

No answer came back to us. I would have asked how the door had been opened if there was no one there to open, but the answer was obvious: magic. The question was whether the opening had been an automatic response or if some magic-user had remotely activated it. For all I knew, we were all alone in here.

"I knew this would be creepy," Ruby said, "but they've gone above and beyond." Raising her voice, she said, *"Above and beyond, assholes!"*

Her voice echoed through the halls, then bounced back to us with greater force than it should have, so much that it rattled the windows and set my eardrums ringing. Gooseflesh popped out along my arms.

"You know what," I said. "Screw this. If they're going to play games, we'll come back later. We don't need this shit."

"Works for me," Ruby said.

We marched back toward the still-open door. Just before I reached it, the huge door slammed shut with a crack that had me reeling back. Blinking, I swore, then jumped forward and pulled desperately at the handles. They didn't budge.

"Allow me," Ruby said.

I stepped back. She muttered a spell, weaving her hands like a dance, and light began to gather on them. At the climax of her casting, she flung her fingers wide. The green light shot off her palms and encased the doorknob, which began to glow.

"It's working!" I said.

Ruby grinned at me. "It's all in—"

Green light flashed off the door, struck her in the chest and flung her through the air. She hit the marble floor and went skidding. I screamed and ran to her, then knelt over her.

"Ruby! Ruby!" I cradled her head and shook her.

She blinked her eyes and lurched up. A huge swell of relief swept through me, and I felt tears burn my eyes. Speaking past the lump in my throat, I said, "Thank God. Are you all right?"

She nodded shakily, but her face had gone pale. "I'm fine." Her voice was rough.

I helped her to her feet and together we glared at the doors. The knob no longer glowed, and I knew it had simply rebounded her power back at her. The spell hadn't worked at all.

"You have anything else that might get us out of here?" I said.

"That was my most powerful unlocking spell."

I bit back a curse and moved to one of the windows. Reaching out a hand toward it slowly, I allowed my senses to feel it, really study it, and almost instantly I could feel the subtle power radiating off of it. Feeling suddenly hollow inside, I turned back to Ruby and shook my head.

"Damn," she said.

I went back to her and hugged her. "I'm so sorry I got you into this, Rubes."

She sniffed. "It's okay, Jade. It was my decision, not yours. We both knew it could be dangerous." Then, lifting her voice again: *"Because you guys are assholes!"*

Her words echoed back at us so powerfully we had to clamp our hands over our ears, and the windows rattled violently.

When the sound had faded, I said, "I'd say we should do that until the windows break, but I think that would kill us first, so maybe not." I gestured toward one of the large doorways leading deeper into the building. "Why don't we go exploring?"

Ruby watched the shadowy doorway as if daring it to act against us, squared her shoulders and raised her chin. "Let's do it," she agreed.

We passed through the doorway and into another large room. Other than the dim light filtering in through the drapes over the windows, the whole place was plunged into darkness. Luckily my half-shifter senses allowed me to see well in the dark, and Ruby had magical tricks up her sleeve that enabled her to see.

"Trying to test us," I guessed as we went along, finding another room, then another, then passing down a long hall.

"I guess. Testing our ability to overcome traps, see in the dark, improvise … all good stuff for a thief to be able to do."

"So you think this is like some sort of initiation?"

"Probably."

I nodded. "Well, they've got another thing coming, because the McClaren sisters—"

Before I could finish the sentence, a huge sword made of what looked like shadow swept toward my head. With a shriek, I ducked, and the blade thunked into the wood paneling of the wall to my right.

The wielder of the blade was a huge giant of shadow, which had either sprung from a nearby doorway or had congealed from the gloom of the building itself. It had the shape of a man, but very tall and gaunt, and its legs were fused together into a sort of tail so that it slithered like a snake.

Even as I was collecting myself, the shadowy swordsman ripped his blade loose of the wall, sending chunks of wood flying. His sword might look insubstantial, but it still packed a hell of a wallop. I wouldn't want to be on the receiving end of that thing.

"This way!" Ruby said.

She grabbed my hand and tugged me down the hall, around the nightmarish apparition and toward a high doorway. Sweat burned my eyes as I followed her, and my heart pounded wildly in my chest. Glancing over my shoulder, I saw the swordsman slithering after us, sword clenched firmly in a claw-like hand.

"Who are you?" I screamed, but the thing didn't respond other than to come closer.

Tearing my hand loose from Ruby's, I grabbed my crossbow off my hip and made sure that a bolt was loaded. I stumbled on the rug and looked up, righting myself. Ruby was a few strides ahead. I pushed myself to go faster. I couldn't hear the footsteps or, more likely, the rasp of scales behind me, but I knew our attacker couldn't be far behind.

Ruby reached the doorway ahead of me and passed through it. I was almost to it when suddenly the door slammed closed, almost smashing me across the nose.

"Fuck!" I said, and pounded on the door.

Ruby smashed on her side, too. "Jade!"

We were trapped, or at least I was. The building had deliberately separated us. With a swear, I wheeled and lifted my crossbow. The swordsman was already raising his blade as he descended on me. I fired. The bolt passed through his chest and kept going, as if he really were only shadow. Damn!

His blade chopped down at my head.

I spun to the side. The blade gouged into the wood of the door, showering chips. I kicked at the bastard's knee while he was trying to get his blade lose, but my foot went right through him.

No fair! I thought. He could hurt me but I couldn't hurt him.

"Run, Jade!" Ruby cried from the other side of the door. "I'll meet you further on. Hey, who are you?" This last part had a strange note to it, and I knew she must be talking to someone—or something—on the other side. *Fuck.* She was being attacked just like I was.

This was a really bad idea. I ducked under the swordsman's arm and ran by him, traveling up the hall I'd just come down. I heard the crack of wood and knew he'd torn his blade lose and would be after me. Where could I go?

I ducked into an open doorway and slammed the door closed behind me.

Backing away from it, I raised my hands and said a spell, magically locking the door and sealing it with a mystical ward.

The shadow swordsman appeared, passing through the door as if it weren't there. With not a sound or a pause, he came straight at me. I turned and ran, passing through one huge, opulent room and then another. At last I saw a set of stairs and ran up them. I paused on the landing to turn and shoot at the monster, enchanting the bolts as I did. These bolts too passed through the thing as if he were made of air.

"Not fair!"

I turned and ran up the rest of the stairs, racking my brains for some solution. What was this thing? I vaguely recalled reading about something similar. Ruby had schooled me on magical avatars and guardians, and I thought this was one she'd instructed me on. One that would be good for a thief to know about.

Think think think!

I reached the head of the stairs. I swung my head, looking one way and another. Neither offered any help. Picking one randomly, I ran to the right.

The swordsman slithered after me, gaining speed as he went. Damn! I couldn't outrun him forever.

All at once, I realized what he must be. A Gorian Construct, woven by Peruvian shadow-magic. A so-called shadowman. Yes indeed, I'd read up on them just in case I ever ran into one.

I slipped into a doorway, ran across it and disappeared around the next doorway before the shadowman could see which way I'd gone. I said a spell to deepen the shadows around me, ducked into another room and slid under a bed. *This had better work.* Shadowmen might be made of shadows, but they couldn't see well in them. Hilarious, right?

And they were powered by … I strained my memory … there it was, yes … Peruvian psych-jewels! Very rare things, and they went for quite a bit on the black market.

I held my breath as a shadow swept across the doorway. I peered out from under the bed, sensing the cold wood against my palms, and felt like a little girl hiding from a boogeyman. But this boogeyman was very real, and very deadly. The thing paused at the doorway. Its head swung this way and that, as if trying to sniff me out. At long last, it slithered up the hall and was gone.

Sucking in a deep breath, I scooted out from under the bed. No sense wandering the halls trying to avoid that bastard. I couldn't hurt him, and neither could I escape. Not only that, but my shadow spell wouldn't last indefinitely. And somewhere Ruby might be needing my help. My only hope was to find the Peruvian psych-jewel that powered the shadowman and deactivate it.

I located the grate over an air duct high up on the wall, dragged a chair over to it and removed it. Pulling myself up and into the vent, I wormed my way forward through the darkness. My heart still pounded wildly, and my hair lay across my forehead, stuck to it with sweat. Filth from the duct clomped to me as I went, glued to me by sweat. I spat it out of my mouth and cursed as I went. I inched my way down one tube, then another, peering through grates as I did, and at last I saw what I was looking for: a shining green jewel floating over a squat pedestal in a small, dark room. The green radiance from the jewel was the only light.

Acting quickly, I used a spell to scan the room for magical boobytraps, finding several, one on the very grate of the duct.

I sprinkled some dust from one of pouches on the grate and intoned, "Ritha-a-lotor!"

The protective ward dissolved. I said another spell to remove the grate, then slid into the room, landing smoothly and silently. I probably would have looked pretty badass, approaching that mystical, dangerous jewel in my cat-burglar outfit, all heroic and awesome, if I hadn't been absolutely covered in crap from the air-conditioning vent. I wished I knew a spell for that!

As I reached for the jewel, saying another spell to deactivate the ward around it, the shadowoman burst into the room. Well, *burst* is probably the wrong word, since he was totally soundless. *Ooze* is probably better.

Okay, so he oozed into the room, passing silently through the one door leading in here. Instantly he fixed on me and rushed in, raising his sword to strike me down.

"I don't think so," I said. I grabbed the jewel with my naked fist, thrust it in the face of the shadowman and screamed "KIVA KUM!"

Green light pulsed out from the jewel, enveloping the shadowman, and he dissolved. Gooey streams peeled away from his main mass and he just wilted away, becoming one with the shadows of the room.

The green light given off by the jewel died, plunging me into blackness.

I sucked in a huge breath, then another, and wiped sweat out of my eyes.

"Well, that sucked," I said.

The room lights flicked on, blinding me, and a voice on some hidden intercom system said, "Well done, Jade McClaren. You have passed the test. Come find me in the study on this floor, just down the hall."

I narrowed my eyes at the ceiling. "Where is my sister?"

Thirty seconds later:

"So glad you could make it," said the figure behind the desk.

Covered in grime, bleeding from a few scrapes I couldn't even remember getting, I had just entered through the study door and was approaching him, and I had to resist the urge to launch myself over his damned desk and strangle him.

"Where's Ruby?" I demanded.

The guy opened his mouth to reply, but just then I heard coughing behind me and turned to see Ruby entering the room. Relief flooded me, and I started to wrap her in a hug, but she waved me off. It was only when I came close that I could smell the stench coming off her. She looked bedraggled, too, her hair messed up and dark splotches on her clothes, along with some burned patches.

"What happened to you?" I said. "That doesn't look like the work of a shadowman."

Ruby's gaze took in the guy behind the desk, then said to me out of the side of her mouth, "I don't want to talk about it."

"Why do you smell so bad?"

"I don't want to talk about it."

"You smell like … poop."

She gritted her teeth. "It was hell monkeys, alright?"

I tried to suppress a burst of laughter. "Hell monkeys? You mean, the little bastards that throw flaming dung?"

She glared hotly at me. Suddenly I realized why she had burnt patches in her clothes, along with that awful smell, and I couldn't help it. I laughed.

"Shut up," she said.

Regaining control of myself, I nodded, and together we rounded on the bastard behind the desk. He regarded us with cool, amused detachment. He was lean and tall, with slicked-back red hair and a red goatee. I'd never seen a ginger with a goatee before, and on him it looked particularly devilish. His whole demeanor was devilish. And he was a natty dresser, too, with a custom Italian suit and a green tie.

"Who the hell are you and what did you just do to us?" I said. "And if we don't like your answer, you're in deep shit."

"Don't say that word," Ruby muttered.

"Talk!" I ordered the guy.

He leaned back in his well-upholstered seat and steepled his fingers beneath his bearded chin. "I'm Gavin Manor, President of the Guild of Thieves. I'm sorry if you suffered any inconvenience."

"Inconvenience?" said Ruby. "Demon monkeys just tried to kill me with flaming crap! *Their own* crap!"

A small smile tugged at the corners of Gavin's mouth. "Fear not, they would not have actually killed you. We have wards to prevent our tests from killing their subjects."

"Tests!" I said. "I knew it. That's why he split us up, Rubes, to test us separately."

"Naturally," Gavin said. "We only allow members into the Guild if they're qualified. We design each test to explore that particular individual's level of talent in their field. For a magically-assisted burglar, a shadowman made sense. For a witch, a more exotic set of foes seemed prudent."

"Exotic?" said Ruby, and took a step forward. "I oughtta—"

"I would measure your next words carefully."

I placed a hand on Ruby's shoulder. She started to shake it off, then sighed and nodded. She didn't finish her sentence.

"Again, I apologize for the inconvenience," Gavin said. "But know that you both passed with flying colors. It would have been unfortunate if only one of you had made it through. I would have hated to've broken up a team."

I made myself count to five, then said, "Now what? Is there a ceremony or something?"

"Don't be foolish. Thieves don't do ceremonies."

"What then?" Ruby said.

Gavin rolled his small shoulders. "Why not … a job?"

Ruby and I glanced at each other.

"A job?" I said.

He smiled, and seemed to relax, just a bit. "That's why you want to sign up, right? To take advantage of the networking opportunities and the resources available in the Guild? Well, we happen to need thieves with just your qualifications. And there's a social tonight where you can mingle and find the job that's right for you."

Ruby plucked a gob of charred dung from her hair. "A social? Like … a party?"

"Exactly!"

Gavin stood and clapped his hands. Instantly the lights brightened.

"Shall I see you at eight?" he said. "I will give you both glamours to wear to hide your real identity."

"What do you think?" I asked Ruby.

She pulled another clump of poop from her hair. "I think that will give me just enough time for a dozen baths."

Chapter 4

"Well, you do smell better," I admitted as we entered the lounge room of the mansion. It was several hours after our meeting with Gavin, and we were all dolled up. We didn't wear our usual club clothes but tight black leather and latex, with lots of zippers. Ruby's zippers were pink, though, which I think took away some of the effect.

Ruby sniffed an arm and wrinkled her nose. "I can still smell it."

"It's in your nose, babe. Like your nostrils. It'll probably take days to get out."

"Great."

Around us gathered thieves and murderers, scoundrels of all descriptions. I saw lean, shadowy figures whispering in a corner, a wily-looking lass trying to sell a hard-eyed woman a set of lockpicking tools, a bald-headed black woman with one white eye giving a speech advertising the benefits of her mercenary group of thieves to a trio of aristocrats. A wizard was obviously on the payroll because colored pyres blazed at regular points throughout the large chamber, throwing shifting waves of multi-colored light on the shadowy proceedings, the only major lights in the room.

"So glad you could make it," said a voice.

Ruby and I turned to see Gavin slide out of the gloom behind us. Something about him gave me the creeps.

Well, okay, it was everything about him.

"We had a clear spot in our calendar," I said.

Ruby gestured around us, then frowned as her gaze fell on a pair of blue-skinned demons speaking at the bar. "Where do we start?" she said, almost in a whisper. "We don't know anyone here. Well, I don't."

"Me neither," I said. "At least no one I recognize yet."

Gavin ushered us to a group of nefarious-looking types, covered in scars and tattoos. Each had a drink in his or her hand but wasn't touching it. Smart. God knew what poisons might be found in a place like this. And these would be the types who knew how to use it.

"Jade and Ruby are new," he said. "Make them welcome."

"Mance," said a gruff fellow sporting orange sideburns. "Welcome."

"Welcome," said a Latino woman with the tattoo of a tiger on her arm. "You can call me Claudia."

We nodded at them, and most of them nodded back. No one offered a hand to shake, and we didn't either. This wasn't that kind of crowd.

Seeing that we were occupied and out of his hair, Gavin melted back into the darkness. We spoke with the group for a bit, getting the lay of the land. Mance knew of a bank job coming up and was trying to feel the others out without getting too specific. Then one of the women started talking about an armored car job she was trying to recruit for. Ruby and I glanced at each other, bored.

"This is getting us nowhere," she told me after a few hours. We'd been going from group to group, trying to find some sign of Nevos. So far no luck.

"I know," I said. "You have a better idea?"

"I guess not. But this sucks. These people freak me out, and so does this place."

I shivered, thinking of the shadowman. Could he have been resurrected, or could there be another one here somewhere? He could be prowling about even now. The Guild of Thieves was really not the sort of organization you wanted to get on the bad side of. And yet here Ruby and I were actively fucking with it on our first day. *Don't poke the bear.*

"Jade," Ruby said, snapping her finger before my eyes. "Earth to Jade, can you hear me?"

"Hysterical," I said. "I was thinking. Let's just get back to it. This party won't last much longer. It's already three in the morning."

"That's another reason this sucks," Ruby said. "We have to stay sober. And there's an open bar."

With a dramatic sigh, she agreed to split up, and we returned to eavesdropping, snooping and listening to various recruiters, sales pitches and doubtful tales of intrigue and adventure. At one point I saw a group of pale women drinking thick red fluid out of wine glasses. My shifter senses detected the scent of blood. *Vampires.* I kept well clear of them. Not only had I had a bad encounter with the undead a few months ago, but I knew my old buddy Vincent Walsh was in league with the bastards. These women could be allies of his.

At last I found a clue. I'd fallen in with a hard-bitten group near the fireplace. One was the bald black woman with one eye. I stood up straighter when one guy said something about the job he was going on about being sponsored by a Fae Lord.

"What's that?" I said. "A Fae?"

The guy nodded. He was short but thick in the chest, and he'd grown a resplendent beard and had thick hair to make up for his height. "That's right," he said. "I probably shouldn't have mentioned it. Forget I said it."

"But that's who you're working for? That's who's trying to set up this job?"

He narrowed his eyes at me. "So what?"

I swallowed. Tucking a strand of hair back behind my ear in my most feminine manner, I batted my eyes and said, "I've always wanted to be under a Fae."

He grinned. "Well, girl, you might want to get in on this. Your specialty is magically-assisted entry and exit, yeah?"

"That's right."

"Then we've got an opening for you. Nothing for that other one, though—your partner, with the hair? If you sign on, that's the last position we need filled."

That would make it easier to break it to her, I thought. The last thing I wanted was to involve Ruby any further. But this really did sound like the best lead I was going to get. If I could get hired by Jim, the short guy, I might just meet his boss. What happened after that I had no idea. I'd cross that disaster when it happened.

"So," he said. "You in?"

I rubbed my chin, as if really thinking it over, then looked up and gave him a measuring glance. "What's the job?"

* * *

"A mansion?" Ruby said. "What's in this mansion?"

I shrugged, which was hard to do driving my flying motorcycle, and I wasn't even sure she could see it. At least we could hear each other. She'd used another one of her noise-dampening spells. Below us the nighttime city scrolled past.

"Who knows," I said. "But it's magically warded and guarded. Obviously Nevos couldn't break in there on his own. He needed help."

"You're assuming it's Nevos."

"True. But it makes sense, right? Nevos was seen nosing around the Guild. Had to be because he needed something stolen."

"Yeah, I guess. And there's probably not two Fae out there hiring thieves from the Guild."

"God, I hope not."

"I wonder what Nevos could want. I mean, it has to be his fallback objective, right? He'd meant to storm the Palace and smash the Fae Lords, but we made sure he didn't have an army. Now what does he want?"

"Hopefully not another army," I said.

"Better not. I wonder how much of Angela's army is left. Any idea?"

"No. Most of them scattered after the battle in the stadium—at least the survivors. A few were caught, though."

"Were do the Fae keep them?" Ruby said.

"Oh, they have a prison somewhere. I've never been there."

"Beware the Dementors."

Black wings pumped to either side of us, stroking the air powerfully. *Damn, I love my ride.* I could see why some people really dug motorcycles.

"What *are* you going to name her?" Ruby said, noticing where my attention was.

"I don't know. But I was thinking … Chromecat."

She laughed, then said, "Actually, that's not bad."

"I don't think so, either."

Suddenly, Ruby stiffened behind me, and her arms locked around my middle.

"What is it?" I said.

She released her hands and glanced all around; I could see her in my rearview. She seemed to be scanning the skies behind us.

"I feel something …"

Fire flared in the blackness of the night directly behind us, spreading out from a central mass. I gasped, watching it in my rearview mirrors. Heart pounding, I craned my head for a moment, but only for a moment. That was enough. What I saw sent a chill coursing down my spine. A huge bird, with maybe a fifteen-foot wingspan, all composed of fire, was bearing straight down on us. It shrieked, and gooseflesh popped out all over my body.

"VERICON MATHRA!" Ruby shouted and waved her wand. Power burst from it.

The huge bird shrieked again, but it pumped its wings to slow itself down, giving us some space, at least for the moment. Watching it out of the corner of my eye via the mirrors, even as I yanked the wheel and banked hard around a corner, I could see that it was some sort of hawk-like bird. A raptor. A bird of prey.

"What the hell?" I shouted over my shoulder.

"I don't know!" said Ruby. "Another test?"

"Lousy Gavin. If this is his doing, he's not getting a Christmas card."

The bird of fire drew in its wings and dove at us, fast. The flames composing it crackled as it sped through the night. I jerked the handlebars, swinging us to the right, and it barreled past, so close I could feel its heat. Its smoke enveloped us. Coughing, I guided us around another turn.

It screamed and flew up at us.

"Na'va correlto!" Ruby said. She threw an azure bolt of energy down on the thing. It veered aside and kept coming. She threw another. Again it dodged and continued toward us. It would strike us at any moment.

I swung the handlebars, jerking us around the corner of a skyscraper, then twisting the bars the other way and sending us around another.

The bird came on.

"Make a net!" I said. "Put it between the buildings!"

"Good idea." She muttered to herself, and I felt a powerful burst of magic behind me. I turned my head to see a magical green spiderweb materialize in the space between two skyscrapers. The bird of flame hit it full on. Flame and smoke crackled, and the web buckled. I held my breath.

"Is it strong enough?" I said.

"We'll find out in a moment."

The bird thrashed, but the net held, and I breathed a sigh of relief. Turing down one corner and another, putting some distance between us and the thing, I felt safer. Who knew how long Ruby's spell-web would hold? She probably didn't know either. I made for our apartment, praying the bird didn't get free and find us there. The last thing we needed was for our enemies to know where we lived—or our friends, either, if Gavin could be considered a friend.

"What was that thing?" I said.

Ruby shook her head. "Beats me. Let's look it up when we get home."

We arrived home in Gypsy Land, the area of town where we lived, fifteen minutes later. I parked on the roof, cast an invisibility spell on the bike—Chromecat? The name was growing on me—and trooped down to our apartment, neat and colorful, with a few knickknacks from our adventures scattered here and there. The whole place was powerfully warded.

"We should be safe now," Ruby said. "Even if that thing gets free, it can't see through these wards."

I poured us both a glass of wine, then took a long sip.

"To nets," I said, lifting my glass.

We clinked glasses and drank.

"Really think it was Gavin?" I said.

"I don't know. It could be anyone we met tonight, or even someone totally random."

"It could've been those vampires. They might have worked for Walsh."

"Maybe. Or it could've been those demons. They looked like they were up to something."

"When *aren't* demons up to something?"

She downed another sip. "Actually, from what you've told about your run-ins with them, I was wondering if there might be something going on there."

I leaned back against the kitchen counter and played a sip of wine around my tongue. Sweet and tart, just the way I liked it. Struggling to pay attention, I said, "Go on."

"You woke up a demon lord in that cemetery."

"We didn't wake him up. He was dead. Angela roused him and his zombie priests to kill me and Davril. We escaped, though."

"Yeah, but Mr. Demon Lord and his buddies are still around. And it was only a couple months after that that we had the homunculi factory incident—all because a woman was doing the bidding of a demon lord."

"You think the two are connected?"

"Maybe."

I shuddered. "Lighten up, sis. Besides, why would they send a fire bird to hunt us down? And what was it?"

We drank and rummaged through our limited magical library, then hit Google. Neither turned up any results, although we thought we had it narrowed down to a magical construct of ancient Assyrian devising. No word on how to discorporate it. The good news was it probably had a short shelf life.

"That's something, anyway," I said. "It's probably faded by now."

She slumped back in her chair, third glass of wine in her hand. "Yep. Couldn't happen to a nicer bird. But I wish I knew who was trying to kill us."

"Would be nice. Well, tell 'em to get in line."

She fixed me with a searching look, and I knew she was about to ask me the question that was really on her mind. I braced myself. Slowly, she said, "Jade, are you going to go through with it?"

"With what?"

"Working with that crew. You know, to steal some magical item from this mansion of yours for Nevos. *That* what."

I let out a breath. "Let me talk to Davril."

Chapter 5

Davril stalked back and forth, mulling on what I'd told him. Morning light turned his hair to beaten gold and made his blue eyes shine. "You're crazy," he said at last.

"I know. But can you think of anything better?"

We were in the Tower of the Shield, in one of the private rooms used for conferences on the third floor. The window afforded a magnificent view of the panorama of the city. Red-tinged sunlight drenched the metropolis, turning everything into molten gold. *Damn*, I thought. *I remember when I couldn't see the tops of the buildings, and now this.* It was a lot to take in. I could understand why Ruby wanted to keep visiting.

Davril turned to me. He was dressed in his clingy athletic clothes, and sweat beaded his forehead and white cotton garments. He had wanted to practice sparring before he would allow me to give my report.

His blue eyes speared me. "What's your game, Jade?"

"My game?"

"You know what I mean. You can't mean to actually help these criminals. That would mean helping Nevos."

"If I'm not part of the team, there goes our eyes and ears. It's going to happen with or without me. Why not be part of it?"

He tapped his chin. "I suppose. But I still think there's something you're not telling me."

"If I am, it's for a reason."

"So there is something."

I allowed myself to flash a grin. "Maybe. But it might not pan out. We'll see. Anyway, it's our best shot, one way or another. Our only chance to get close to Nevos."

His voice lowered an octave. "You'll be on your own, Jade. I ... won't be there to protect you."

"I ... I know. But I'll be fine." I placed one hand on my hip and batted my eyes at him. "I *will* miss you, though, handsome."

He said nothing, just stared at me. My heart went *thump-thump*.

"And who knows?" I said. "Maybe Nevos will be cute."

One corner of Davril's mouth quirked, and humor flashed in his eyes. I thrilled to see it. You never knew with Davril.

"Oh, I'm sure he would say so," Davril said. "But really, Jade. Be careful. Nevos is dangerous. Remember, he caused the downfall of not just my kingdom but the entire Fae. Our world is completely in thrall to the Shadow now, thanks to him."

The old need for a cigarette came on me suddenly, but I forced it back down. It had been years since my last smoke, and I meant to keep it that way.

"I'll remember," I said. My limbs still burned from the workout, and my blood boiled from sparring with Davril. I could smell his sweat, too, clean and lightly spiced with a hint of musk. It was sexy as hell.

"I'll miss you, too," I said.

He cleared his throat. "You know how to call for us when you need us, right?"

By *us*, he meant the full might of the Fae Knights. I might be going undercover amongst the Guild of Thieves, but I could summon an army whenever I wanted. *Just like James Bond.*

"Got it," I said.

He took a step closer to me, so close I could feel his heat. "Be careful, Jade. Come back to me."

Gulp.

"I will." I hesitated. Was now the time to resume what we'd started yesterday? I waited for him to make the first move, but he just stood there, gazing down at me.

Eventually, he shook himself, then moved past me, our shoulders just brushing, to the door. "Time for showers," he said.

Is there enough room in there for two? I almost said. I knew he wanted to keep our relationship professional, but I also knew there was something there, and the longer it built up the more frustrated I was getting. I knew it might be bothering him, too. *Heh*, I thought. *I've got him hot and bothered.* Only I was, too, damn it.

Our gazes lingered on each other just for a moment as he turned at the door, then he moved out of sight. I let out a long sigh. *My shower's going to be cold.*

Afterwards, I found my flying motorcycle in the hangar and stroked her handlebars lovingly. "Are you ready to go for a ride, Chromecat?"

She didn't exactly bounce up and down, but I thought I sensed a swell of excitement from her. I also thought she liked the name. I did. *Wait till I tell Jessela.* I hadn't been able to hang out with my female Fae Knight friend in almost a week. We would have to do something about that soon. I had a new bottle of Fae wine I'd acquired with my last paycheck, and I wanted her to teach me the finer points of the stuff. It was as good an excuse as any to get plastered with a girlfriend.

I hopped astride Chromecat (*May as well start thinking of you that way*, I thought at the bike) and took to the skies. The wind streamed my hair out behind me and I relished the feeling of the sunlight on my skin. As the city tilted below me to every small turn of the handlebars, I smiled wide. *This* was living! My fire and my wings may have been stolen from me by Vincent Walsh, but by God I had new wings now. Black ones, sure, but they kicked ass.

I'd never been to my destination, but I'd heard about it, and I followed the directions Gavin had given (ha ha, Gavin and given) me into a seedy area of town, then found the rusty building indicated. Sure enough, lights and music blazed from an appropriately seedy-looking rooftop bar. They were starting to become popular, what with the rise in people using dirigibles and zeppelins. I saw a few ratty dirigibles tied up at the dock, but not many. The clientele here weren't a group of fliers, then, but just liked rubbing scuffed elbows with them. And I doubted the fliers were on the up and up.

That included me.

I flew Chromecat down and landed her on the roof, then glanced in a mirror to make sure my glamour was in place. It was. Gavin had given that to me, too, in order to ensure that I could protect my identity from my new associates. A stranger's face stared back at me from the side-view mirror, but it was presentable enough. It would only last a few hours before fading. The rest of me was my normal self, clad in my black cat burglar outfit complete with a utility belt packed with spellgredients. I was ready for action.

"Want me to tie her up for you?" a rough-looking guy said, coming over. He meant Chromecat.

"No thanks," I said, turning off the engine. I ran a hand through my hair, smoothing it out. "I'll get it."

Hopping off, I tied the bike off. No way I trusted these yay-hoos. I hunched my back unconsciously as I entered the bar, its neon-spiced shadows falling over me. Wouldn't want to come here at night, I thought. It was about noon, and this place was thick with shadows and hushed conversations. Thuggish and larcenous folk of all descriptions spoke and drank and laughed all around. Some brooded darkly in corners. One fingered a knife. A guy dressed like a pilot was chatting up a young woman at the bar while another guy tried to buy him a beer.

I found Hela and the others at a table near the bar. She was the leader of our raid, a green goblin with a scaly crest sticking up from her head like a Mohawk. I'd never met a goblin before but knew they came from the Fae Lands. Her kind were enemies of the Fae, generally. She'd fled her homeworld, though, so I didn't know where her loyalties lay.

"Glad you could find the place," she grunted to me.

The others chuckled. There were three of them, and they were a hard lot. One was a huge guy with a red Afro. Another was a Latina woman with silver hair, eyelashes and tight silver clothes, including boots. I was instantly jealous. The third was a medium-sized, sinewy black guy with glowing green Xs tattooed over his eyelids, so that I saw an X on each eye every time he blinked.

"Yeah, well, I'm a busy gal," I told Hela.

They hadn't bothered to wait for me to start eating lunch. Fortunately, the waiter, a guy dressed as a biker, came over and took my order—cheeseburger. I do love a cheeseburger, and this probably wasn't the crowd to indulge my periodic love of green things in front of.

"We were just going over the plan," Hela said.

The sinewy guy with the Xs on his eyelids tapped a piece of paper on the table. It looked blank.

"I don't see anything," I said.

"Fisa mumlatta," he intoned, and waved a hand in front of my eyes.

I blinked, the image on the page slowly coming into view. Nice. A spell that could mask sensitive information from prying eyes. And this was definitely the right place to use it.

"Can you see it now?" he said.

"Yeah." I studied him with new appreciation. Like the others, he hadn't been at the Guild meeting earlier, so this was my first introduction to him.

"Lux, they call me," he said.

"Jade."

We nodded at each other.

"And this is Robespierre," Hela said, indicating the big guy with the frizzy red hair. "And this Sathaba." She gestured to the Latina in silver.

I waved at them. They cautiously lifted their hands to me. I wondered if they wore glamours, too, or if I was seeing the real "them".

My cheeseburger arrived as we went over the plans again, and I munched on it as I studied the op. Hela pointed to various points on the picture, indicating the different stages of the plan. I admired the image. *Beautiful.* The picture showed a zeppelin, but no ordinary one. The airship depicted was a mansion in the sky. A wizard lived there. A dangerous one. Even though the air was reasonably warm, and the meat was hot in my mouth, I felt a chill. What we were about to do was crazy—break into the aerial lair of a powerful magic-user. *I'm not getting paid enough for this shit.* Then again, my real payment was to get closer to Nevos.

Somehow.

"Any questions?" Hela asked when she was done, her gaze going around to each of us. We all shook our heads. I hoped I didn't look as blank as I felt. The truth was I'd only half been paying attention. The other half of my brain had been hatching my double-cross.

"Good," she said. "Then I guess we're ready to go."

"Ready," said Sathaba.

"Ready," said Lux.

"Excuse me?" I said. "Ready for what?"

Hela frowned at me with her weird green face, and the scales on her head pulsed red in anger. "Weren't you listening?" she said. "We're leaving now."

"*Right* now?"

She gnashed her sharp teeth. "Yes," she said, visibly repressing her anger. Sheesh, goblins could get mad easily. "Right now."

Robey laughed at me, flashing brown teeth. "Don't mind the newbie, Hell. She was just too busy admirin' me to pay attention."

"As if," I said. Although the truth was that his gray sweater under that tattered bomber jacket was pretty tight, and I could see that he was built damn well. I wasn't sure about that frizzy hair, though.

"Is there a problem?" Hela asked me, and I knew she meant that if I was going to back out, it better be now. We really were leaving right now. That had *not* been part of the original plan.

"Er, no," I said. *Glad I came in my suit.* "I mean, let's go, already. What are we waiting around for?" *Some excuse to back out of this, maybe.*

Instead, Hela threw a wad of cash down on the table. Evidently she was paying for us all. Hell, if I'd known that I would've ordered the fries. When she stood and moved toward one of the doors, the rest of us followed. She led the way to a docking bay, where a dirigible was tied up, straining against its cords as the wind bobbed against it. Its pilot smoked a cigarette and leaned against the railings. He stood straighter when Hela approached.

"Time to go," she said.

He nodded. "We're ready."

We turned out to be him and one crewman. We boarded, and they cast off. I wobbled on my feet as the deck swayed beneath me, then clutched at a railing—a gunwale, I guess—for support. We rose above the rooftop bar, then the surrounding buildings, and I held back a swear when I saw the city streets move beneath us. This was different from being in Lady Kay somehow, or even Chromecat. We were in a *ship*. In the *air*. It was pretty cool.

I felt butterflies in my belly as we rose above the city, drifting gracefully and purposefully. Wind misted my eyes, but I loved it. The rocking of the deck made me a little nauseous, but I pushed it down.

"First time in dirigible?" Sathaba said, coming to lean on the gunwale next to me. Her silver eyelashes flashed in the sunlight.

I swallowed. "Yeah."

She stretched luxuriously, and I wondered if she was trying to draw my attention to her chest. It was nice, I had to admit, but I didn't swing that way. "I love the air," she said. "Especially dirigibles and zeppelins. There's just something special about them."

"Uh-huh."

"Something wrong?"

I shrugged. "Just thinking about the job."

"What about it?"

"It just doesn't make sense to me. I mean, I know we're supposed to steal something, this item, from the air mansion, but what does it do? Who is it for?"

She studied me, silver lashes lowering. "You ask a lot of questions for a thief."

"Hey, I'm a cat burglar. We're curious." I tried a smile on her that I had been told was winning, but either I'd been misled or she was a hard sell.

"Don't be too curious," she said and moved off.

I let out a breath. *That's Lesson Number One*, I told myself. *Don't give yourself away, toots.* If these guys knew why I was really here, they would string me up in five seconds flat. Or maybe Hela would just eat me. I'd heard goblins ate human flesh. Hopefully that was just an exaggeration. Either way, I had to remember that I was now officially an undercover agent.

As we plowed through the air, I avoided talking to the others as best I could. Part of it was because I didn't want to give myself away. I'd proven just how much I sucked at hiding my motives. That was one thing about my profession; it was a solitary one. Teamwork wasn't part of my skillset. In order to get along with a team, sometimes you had to lie, and I wasn't as good at that as I needed to be. Ruby might think otherwise, but she was wrong.

The other reason I avoided the others was to keep from getting close to them. After all, soon I might have to betray them. They wanted the item (whatever that was; its actual description was something Hela wasn't sharing) for themselves, or at least their employer. But if we got it, I knew it was Hela that would hand it over to him, not the whole group. She would get the credit and the alone time with Nevos, if that's who it was, and I was pretty sure it was.

Somehow *I* had to be that person. I had to get him alone for my own purposes.

That meant I had to get the item for myself … and do something to the rest of the group to ensure they couldn't come after me until it was too late. Well, we were going into a wizard's lair. Hopefully I could turn something there to my advantage. If it didn't get me killed, that was.

Or if something else didn't do the job first.

Chapter 6

"There it is," Hela said.

She stood at the bow, staring through a set of magically-enhanced binoculars. We were just passing a stately zeppelin, one of several that we'd seen, but that's not what she was talking about. Her focus was on a blob just coming into view on the horizon.

I and the others joined her.

"You sure?" said Lux.

Hela tapped her binoculars, drawing attention to the ancient runes painted on them. *Magically augmented binocs*, I thought. *Cool*. I wondered if they could do X-ray vision. I wouldn't mind seeing what Robespierre was packing, if you know what I mean. Because I can explain.

"I'm sure," Hela said.

"We'll be on them in five minutes," said the pilot.

Hela nodded her chin at Lux. "Ready?"

He nodded. "I'm ready."

"For what?" I said.

"To cast a spell of invisibility."

"I can do one of those," I said.

He smiled, humoring me. "Maybe. But I've made quite a study of the art, Jade. It's, ah, kind of a specialty of mine."

"You would've known that if you'd been paying less attention to me and more to the briefing," Robes told me, flexing his bulging biceps.

"Well, I can't help it," I said. "I mean, just *look* at those things."

He laughed, and we shared an honest grin. I was beginning to think these guys weren't so bad. Damn it. Betraying them would be a lot easier if I could dislike them more.

"Do it," Hela told Lux.

He muttered some words into his cupped palms, and an orange energy began to glow inside them, filtering through his flesh and bones. His chant grew louder and he spread his hands wide. The energy flooded out and enveloped the entire ship. As it washed over me, my ears popped.

"Well done," Hela said.

I peered at another zeppelin we were just nearing. "So they can't see us at all?" I said.

"That's right," Lux said. "Even with sophisticated magics, we should be invisible."

"Nice."

He stood straighter and gave a courtly bow. "Why, thank you."

Turning to Robes, I said, "So what's your specialty?"

He flexed his fists, drawing my attention to tattoos stretching across his knuckles. When he made a fist, they glowed slightly. I nodded. His strength had been magically boosted.

"I'm muscle," he said needlessly.

"Of a very sophisticated kind." I couldn't help but be admiring. Such spells were dangerous, and they only bonded with people of strong wills. If they didn't bond with you, they could kill you. He had survived real hazards to do what he'd done. I realized that his boastful attitude wasn't just bluster but was well earned.

"And you?" I asked Sabetha.

She fluttered her silver eyelids at me, and instantly I felt dizzy.

"Mesmerism," she said. When she stopped batting her eyes, I stood steadier. "In case we encounter any guards Robes can't clobber, I'll put them to sleep."

"A non-lethal crew of criminals," I said, admiringly. Damn it, I really hadn't expected to like them. But the bitter truth was that if I was ever tempted to join an actual gang, this would be it.

"What's *your* deal?" Robes asked me. "*Tell* me it's sex magic. You'd be a hell of a distraction."

"Lay off her," Hela told him, and he sighed.

"I've been on my own for a long time," I said. "I'm kind of a jane-of-all-trades. But I think Gavin put me down as an expert at penetrating magical wards, like for safe-cracking."

"You'd better be what he said you were," Hela told me. "Where we're going, we can expect powerful wards."

"Just what *are* we stealing, anyway?"

"You don't need to know that."

"Alright, your turn," I said. "What's your specialty?"

She narrowed her eyes. "Management."

I swallowed. "Oh. Good. You look like a … manager."

She relaxed, just a bit, and I breathed out. "Also, goblin magic," she said. "Not that there's that much use for it in this world. And I'm not bad in a fight."

I could have guessed that much.

"We're there," Lux said. He stood beside the pilot, staring at something over my shoulder. I turned and shuddered to see us approaching the zeppelin that was our target: the wizard's aerial mansion. And it was truly a mansion, although one unlike any I'd ever seen before. Gleaming polished wood, all glimmering of brass fixtures and sparkling with multi-faceted windows, it hung suspended from the massive burgundy envelope. Jutting balconies thrust out from the sweeping sides of the ship, and eerie lights burned from the windows, which twinkled like chandeliers.

"Wow," I said.

Robes whistled. "That's some pad."

"Suck it up," Hela told us. To the pilot, she said, "Bring us in."

He nodded and turned us broadside to the zeppelin, then brought us closer. His mate threw ropes across to the railing of a balcony and tied us off. We were now moored to the mansion.

Hela gestured from me to the window. "I believe you are our expert on window wards."

"That's me," I agreed. "An expert of wards of all types. A ward wonder, really."

"Just get it open."

I wondered if all goblins had crap senses of humors. Or maybe I just wasn't that funny. Hiding a sigh, I moved toward the balcony, stretching out my palms to feel the magical energies it radiated. I winced. This place was heavily protected, Hela had been right. Its wards were thick, strong and deadly. Just like Ruby's coffee.

"Can you do this?" Hela asked me, apparently sensing my unease.

I patted my belt of spellgredients. "Gavin gave me access to the Guild's magical storeroom. He said the commission he'd get off this job would more than cover the loss of his rare spellgredients. With these things, I can get us in." *If we don't all die first*, I didn't add.

I mixed a few of the spellgredients in a small stone dish, muttering spells over them, then flung the resulting dust at the energy barrier. It shimmered. Stretching out my hand again, I could sense the change.

"Follow me," I said. "The hole I created in the ward isn't very wide."

Ducking, I slipped through the opening and alit on the balcony. Hela followed first, then Robes, Sabetha and Lux. The pilot and his mate stayed on the dirigible. They were our getaway drivers.

Knowing my job wasn't done, I went to the door of the balcony and disarmed the ward there, too. The others followed me into the darkened interior, and Lux closed the door behind us, then said a spell to make us invisible. The shadows deepened around us. We'd really done it. We were inside the wizard's mansion. The air was cool, and the small hairs on the nape of my neck stood at rigid attention. *This was a bad idea.* Surely there were easier ways to get to Nevos.

"This way," said Hela.

I jumped at the sound of her voice. Was she crazy to talk at a normal speaking level? There could be guards here!

Seeing my shock, she tapped her throat, where a red jewel glimmered. "Goblin magic," she said. "I can speak and only be heard by those I wish. The rest of you, speak in whispers. I can mask the sounds of others, but only a little."

Keeping her head low, she led the way down a hall, around a turn, then ascended a polished-wood staircase. The rest of us followed close behind, keeping our heads low and our footsteps light. We might be cloaked, but the dude that owned this place was no pushover. Even his guards were probably magically powered. The place was posh, that was for sure. Everything was made of the finest materials, from silk pillows to teak doors, from oak paneling to granite counters. I had to admit the wizard had taste. When we passed windows, the panorama of the city was laid out below us, and I had to resist a gasp of awe. *I might have to get a zeppelin.*

It was clearly a wizard's home, that was for sure. The very air crackled with power. Strange artifacts on shelves seemed to blur and twist, the laws of physics being warped in their vicinity. But although the place was handsome, it was cold. No family photos, no funky art or throw pillows. It was all browns and golds and silvers, and the only artwork was abstract or surreal. The floor seemed to hum beneath my feet, and I could detect the subtle rocking of the zeppelin. Still, it was easy to forget we were in a mansion flying through the skies, at least until we hit another window.

Those got fewer, though. Hela led us deep into the interior of the mage's lair, and I wondered how she knew where we were going. They must have been planning this for a while—ever since Nevos came to this world, anyway. Just what was he after?

"Hold," Hela said, and drew to a stop, crouching. The rest of us followed suit.

Ahead of us, a pair of long shadows draped the ground through an archway. Then the men the shadows belonged to stepped through. Dressed in flowing black robes, each held a black wand in his hand. Wizards. But I somehow knew that neither of these were the mansion's owner. These were guards.

As one, they swung their gazes toward us.

"Run and die," said one.

"Shit," said Robespierre. "They see us."

Hela stood, and the wizards' attention went to her.

"Interesting," said the other wizard. "I haven't seen a goblin in awhile."

"Should we keep her as a trophy?" said the other.

The first one smiled. "Maybe her head."

They raised their wands toward her.

"Wait," said Sabetha. She glided forward, a nimble, voluptuous form glittering of silver. The wizards' wands turned to her. "You don't want to hurt us." As she spoke, she batted her eyes.

The first wizard blinked. "Don't ... want ..."

"Fool," said the other. "She's laying a spell." Glaring at Sabetha, he said, "That's the last mistake you'll ever make."

Energy gathered on the tip of his wand. He was about to incinerate her. But Hela was already in motion. A flick of her fingers and a tiny blade flashed through the air. It struck the mage in the throat. He collapsed backward, blood spurting. The wand fell inert to the floor. The other mage started to turn to him, but Sabetha stepped forward and touched him on the hand. He turned back to her.

"You want to go to sleep," she purred.

He smiled tiredly. "I think I'll take a nap."

She pointed to a corner. "That looks like a nice spot."

"Yes, a very nice spot …"

He lowered himself into the corner, closed his eyes and instantly began to snore. Sabetha snatched up his wand and tucked it away. The other wizard had stopped moving, and his blood trickled onto his chest and began to soak into his clothes. Sabetha stared down at him regretfully.

"He was an asshole," she said, "but he had a strong will."

"Stronger than Lux's concealment spell," Hela said.

"Sorry about that," Lux said. "But you know how it is. No spell is a hundred percent. Keen minds and powerful magic can pierce any illusion, especially if luck isn't on your side."

"Let's hope it's on our side the rest of the way," said Robespierre.

Hela pushed on, and we pressed close behind her, hoping Lux's spells would hold up better if we stayed in a bunch. At last we entered what looked like a study, and Hela moved to the far wall. She removed a painting of vaguely disquieting abstract symbols, revealing a gleaming safe.

"You're up," she said to me.

I nodded and moved forward. My fingers shook as I reached out my hand to feel the wards on the safe, and my heart thudded in my chest. Shit had gotten real, and now I wasn't sure who I was more afraid of, Hela and her gang or the wizard and his. Hela's gang might try at being peaceful, but when push came to shove they could be just as deadly as anyone. And I didn't like the thought of disappointing her. I doubted she gave a lot of second chances.

"Gehaim mala," I chanted, using a stone engraved with ancient runes to carve through the magical barrier I'd sensed. I could feel it folding away. When it was completely parted, I moved to the safe. In less than two minutes, I had it open. Darkness gaped where the door had been, and I peered in, honestly curious.

Then, suddenly, the world changed for me. Everything became clear, and also terrifying. Because sitting right there in the shadows of the safe was *the golden antler of a Hind.*

"Are you all right?" Robespierre said, coming to stand beside me.

Breathlessly, I nodded. My eyes fixed on that antler. Could it be? Could this place really belong to ... *him?* Because the last time I'd seen that damned thing, it had been in the possession of my arch-nemesis, the evil mage Vincent Walsh.

"You look white as a ghost," Sabetha said.

I shook my head. "Never mind. Is that thing what we're after?"

Surprisingly, Hela reached her green hand into the safe, shoving the antler out of the way, and grabbed up another item instead. Before I could get a look at it, she'd stuffed it in a pouch at her waist and had turned back around.

"Let's go," she said.

She moved out the door, and the others followed her. I stayed where I was, my attention returning to the safe. To the antler. Walsh had gone through a lot of trouble to get that thing, and I just knew that couldn't be a good thing for my side. I reached out a hand toward the antler, meaning to steal it back, but just then the safe door slammed shut. Startled, I jumped. I tried to open the safe again, but it was frozen fast.

Weird.

"Well?" said Sabetha at the door. "You coming?"

Reluctantly, I followed. Sweat burned my eyes as we made our way back through the halls toward the dirigible. My gaze darted all around. *Dear God, that was the golden antler! This is the house of Vincent Walsh!* I'd been searching for him for so long, and now I'd accidentally stumbled into his very home.

"So what was your deal back there?" Robes asked me. "You looked freaked. Shit, you still do."

"Nothing. Just let's hurry. This place is bad news."

"Why do you say that?" said Lux.

"I ... think I know the guy that owns it."

Hela turned to face me. "Who do you think it is?"

I swallowed. "No one."

She resumed walking, and we followed. I positioned myself close to Hela—close to her magic pouch. Somehow I had to steal that thing, or what was inside it. I had to take it, slip away, evade the others or trap them, make my way to the dirigible, somehow find Nevos ...

I resisted a sigh. It was no easy task I'd set myself. But what were my alternatives?

"Almost there," said Hela over her shoulder. "Just around this—"

We rounded the bend to find a golem blocking our path.

Chapter 7

The golem stretched almost to the ceiling and was as wide as two linebackers side by side. Sadly it wasn't as sexy. Lumpen and misshapen, the clay-made thing was shaped vaguely like a man, but it was crude and primal. Smoldering fire burned in its eye sockets. *Bastard must weigh a thousand pounds*, I thought. *Wonder it doesn't crash through the floor.*

"It's blocking off the route to the balcony," Sabetha said. "Lux, can it see us?"

As if to answer, the golem took a lumbering step toward us. The floor jumped beneath my feet when it moved.

"Shit," I said. My plans to steal the pouch would have to wait.

"You have something of my master's," said the golem, and its voice shook like thunder, rattling my eardrums. Hela gnashed her teeth and Robes stuck fingers in his ears.

"Shut up!" I said. I grabbed up my crossbow and shot the thing, right in the chest. My bolt splintered.

"You are getting sleepy," Sabetha said, going before the golem.

It swiped a huge arm at her head. Eyes wide, she danced back. Mesmerism wasn't going to work on this thing.

Robes gritted his teeth and stepped forward. He smacked a fist into a meaty palm. "Let's do this, asshole!"

It swung at his head. He ducked under the swing, then hammered a blow into the golem's abdomen. The runes in his fists glowed as he struck. The golem staggered back. Grinning, Robes hit it again, then again. With each blow, the golem stepped backward. Then one of its arms hit Robes in the side, throwing him against the wall with great force. I heard a *crack* and Robes slid to the floor, dazed. Blood ran from the corner of his mouth, and one of his arms stuck out at an awkward angle.

"Fucker broke my arm," he said.

I put my body under his good arm and helped him up, and together we staggered back to the others. The floor jumped beneath my feet, and the reek of minerals and clay grew stronger. The golem was right on our heels.

"Run!" I said.

The others didn't need to be told twice. Together we fled back through the halls, one step ahead of the magical construct—the homeowner's version of a guard dog, maybe. Walsh's hound. I was sure this place was his. I couldn't imagine him selling the antler to anyone so soon after acquiring it.

"You will give it back or die," thundered the golem. A crystal vase on an ornate holder shattered at the sound.

Instinctively I ducked just as the golem's huge fist passed where my head had been half a second before. I felt the whoosh of the air against my head. The fist pounded into the wall next to me, showering splinters. One sliced my cheek as I ran. That had been too close. Robes swore beside me.

Hela turned into a broad doorway and the rest of us poured through it after her.

The golem blasted through the doorway, throwing chunks of wood and masonry far out into the room. It bellowed loudly, making my belly quiver.

There was no hope of stealing Hela's mystery bag now. No hope of stranding them here while I slipped back to the ship and away. I needed to stick with the others for sheer survival, and even that was in serious question.

"Here," Robes grunted, and removed his arm from around me. He could run on his own now that he'd caught his breath. It had been his arm that had been hurt, not his legs, after all.

Freed, I could run faster. I didn't, though. I didn't want to leave Robes behind. He'd already sacrificed enough for us. *Don't get soft*, I told myself. Just moments ago I'd been looking for some way to betray him and the others. Of course, that had been before his big heroic maneuver.

Hela half-turned and hurled a green fireball at the golem. Both Robes and I ducked as it flashed over our heads. I turned to see it smash the golem in the chest. The impact exploded brightly, showering us all with green sparks and smoke. For a moment I couldn't see the golem at all, and I dared to hope it had been destroyed. Then it lumbered out of the smoke, its eyes ablaze, and the floor trembled (just like my belly) at its heavy tread.

Hela issued some goblin-ish swear and said, "I can't stop it."

"Me either," said Lux. None of the rest of us had to say a word. If we could've stopped it, we sure as hell would have.

We ran through another doorway, made a turn, fled along a hall, then ducked through a narrow door. Hela meant to lose the golem, but he stayed right on our heels. If he could breathe I would have felt his hot breaths on the back of my neck, he was that close. Instead my own breaths grew hotter, and more labored.

"Tell the ship to meet us on the southeast balcony!" I said. I was an old hand at bossing around getaway drivers, although usually it was Ruby.

Hela didn't bother to argue. Yanking out her walkie-talkie, she hit a button and relayed my suggestion.

"On it," said the pilot.

We made another turn, fleeing down a broad hall. I didn't remember it. It seemed wider than the rest and carpeted in rich crimson. Ornamental brass gongs lined the walls. I knew by the shaking of the floor that the golem was still right on our heels.

Suddenly I tripped. Robes stumbled, too, and we both leaned against each other to right ourselves. Eyes wide, I looked down to see that the ground was scrolling beneath our feet. The whole floor was moving.

"Holy shit!" Sabetha said.

My heart hammered rapid-fire in my chest. The floor beneath me moved like a treadmill, cycling backward … toward the golem. Gasping, I glanced over my shoulder. The golem lurched toward us, somehow completely unaffected by the treadmill floor.

"Goddamn wizard house," Robes grunted. "Should've known there'd be a magic floor!"

It was a damn good booby-trap, that was for sure. The golem would be on me and Robes any second. Thinking fast, I reached into the pouches of my utility belt, mixed a couple of spellgredients in my palm and flung them at the golem's feet. As the powder sailed through the air, I said, *"Victum roglis!"*

The cloud of dust wrapped around the golem's legs, becoming a gummy gray substance. The golem slowed, but I knew that would only delay it for a few moments. Robes and I ran faster, but we only progressed a few inches on the magical treadmill the floor had become.

"What's causing this?" Lux said. "Find it and we might be able to get out of this."

"There!" Sabetha said, pointing to a portrait hanging from the wall at the end of the corridor. At seeing the image, my blood ran cold. It was Vincent Walsh, there could be no doubt. His cold, handsome face with his full, sensuous lips and haughty eyes stared out at us smugly, seeming to bask in our plight. Weird ruins jutted behind him in the background. On his right hand glimmered a ring inset with a black jewel. *The ring!* Just seeing a picture of it made my breath catch in my throat. The real-life version of that ring held my fire. The piece of my missing self.

"Destroy it!" Sabetha said.

Hela waved a hand, and a spear appeared there. It must have been miniaturized and stored on her person, just like she'd hidden away whatever she'd stolen from Walsh's safe. She cocked her arm and flung it with all her strength. The goblin spear, which was black and sported wicked edges, flew through the air and impaled Vincent Walsh's image right through the chest. If only that had been the real Walsh.

Instantly the ground quit moving beneath our feet. We all stumbled forward, righting ourselves. Then, breathless, we followed Hela to the end of the hall, turned left, then made our way through one corridor and another.

"You saved our lives," Hela told me as we paused to peer around a corner. Seeing no one and nothing was waiting for us there, we continued on.

"You did, too," I said.

Lux consulted with his magical compass, finding the southeast balcony, and soon we were flinging open the balcony door and rushing out onto it. The dirigible waited for us, the pilot at the helm and the mate standing at the gunwale with a shotgun, meaning to help us repel any pursuers.

As if on cue, the ground shook beneath our feet, and I flinched to hear the roar of the golem.

"Hurry!" said the pilot.

We scrambled over the gunwale and the mate cast us off, then spun to the doorway. The golem, wider than the doorframe, blasted through it, showering splinters, and part of me rejoiced at the thought of Vincent Walsh having to clean up after his automaton. But then the golem raced toward us with shocking speed, and the half-smile that had been forming on my face withered.

The mate fired at the golem, but the shotgun blast, just like Hela's goblin magic attack, didn't even slow the thing down.

The dirigible shot away from the balcony just as the golem reached it. It lashed the air and roared, but we were out of range.

"Ha!" I said, and gave it the finger.

I turned to Sabetha to see her grinning at me. Lux gave me a high-five, then a low-five. Robes embraced me in a crushing hug, then swore and separated, making a rueful face at his injured arm. Hela set to dressing it with her magic. My blood sang. I was part of a badass crew, and we'd just made off with some prize loot taken from a hated foe.

But what the hell was I going to do now? I watched the little black sack that contained the mystery item sway back and forth from Hela's waist as she worked on Robes. So close but yet so far.

My reverie was broken by the dirigible's first mate. He was pointing over my shoulder, his face growing tight and his eyes fixed. "Guys, I think we have a problem," he said.

I turned. I half-expected to see Walsh barreling down on us in his dragon form. It wasn't that bad, but it wasn't good. The zeppelin that was Walsh's home was turning, its prow swinging to face us. As I watched, it lurched forward right toward us.

"Shit," I said.

"That wizard guard must have woken up," Lux said.

"Should've killed him," Hela said, straightening from her attentions on Robespierre.

"Think he knows we took that?" I said, hitching my chin at Hela's bag.

"Good bet he does."

"Guess he's piloting that thing," said Lux.

"Or directing the pilot," said the pilot of our ship, cigarette jutting from one corner of his lips. Eyes flinty, he jerked the wheel and mashed levers, shooting his craft in the opposite direction of the zeppelin. This didn't appear to be his first time running from danger.

The zeppelin followed, sunlight winking on its burgundy envelope and curved wooden balconies. It grew closer with every second. Damn, it was fast.

"Think it'll call the cops?" said Sabetha.

I shook my head. "Guys like him have their own law."

Robes lifted his eyebrows. He sprawled on a bench, the sleeve rolled back from his wounded arm. A clear gel glistened on the red lines of his fracture, and the wound seemed to be healing even as I watched. "Just what is it with you and the owner of that zep?" he said.

"Never mind. Just be glad he was away when we came by. And you'd better hope that guard mage hasn't called him back home. I'm praying the guard will want to recover the item before he does." Grimly I added, "His life might hinge on it."

"Hang on," said the pilot.

He mashed another gear and the ship rocketed forward. The zeppelin started to diminish behind us, then increased its pace. The pilot ground his jaw, hit another button, and I had to grab onto the gunwale as we blasted forward.

"Maybe I can cloak us," Lux said. He weaved another spell, and the dirigible and its occupants grew hard for me to see.

The zeppelin drove on, indomitable.

"Give it up," Sabetha taunted him. "That guard is hip to your tricks."

The pilot turned us into the valley between skyscrapers, removing us from the line of sight of the zeppelin. Sweat sheening his face, he yanked the wheel, plunging us down a narrower lane, then an even narrower one.

"Now try your spell," Hela told Lux.

As the pilot brought the ship to a stop in mid-air, Lux wove another incantation. I helped, deepening the shadows around us. For what seemed like hours, we stayed there, my heart pounding like a crazy drum, sweat stinging my eyes, as the zeppelin hunted us. Maybe Walsh joined in the pursuit, I didn't know. I didn't see his dragon form flying overhead, thank God. Once, though, I saw the shape of the zeppelin rolling by overhead, searchlights sweeping from its underside.

I tensed, then jumped as I felt Sabetha holding my hand tightly. I squeezed back. Both our heads were craned up, staring at the zeppelin, dreading the fall of its searchlight on our little alley.

Then the zeppelin vanished from sight, and we all breathed out.

Lux grinned. "See? I got this."

Hela shook her head. "Good job, guys. Let's give it another few minutes, then I'll have Max drop us off back at the bar. Gavin will send out the payments after I've cleared the job with him."

We nodded our agreement, and in ten minutes the pilot, Max, was taking us back to the rooftop bar we'd begun this misadventure from. We saw no sign of the zeppelin, although I noticed Max kept the ship low and stuck to the small alleys where Lux's and my spells seemed to work better. Max brought us up only when we arrived at the bar, then lit another smoke while his mate tied the ship off at the marina. We thanked him and hopped out of the ship, Hela slipping him a wad of cash.

"Maybe we should have a drink before we split up," I suggested to the group. The truth was I just wanted to delay us breaking up so I could figure out some way of getting the bag. But I have to admit part of me didn't want to break up the band so soon. Damn it all, despite everything, it had actually been kind of fun. I felt a little bad for the wizard who had died, but he served Walsh, and I knew that anyone who knowingly served that bastard must be kind of a bastard, too, so I didn't feel *too* bad.

"Can't," said Lux. "I've got a thing."

"Me, too," said Sabetha.

I sighed. The other members of the group nodded their farewells at each other, and me, then broke up. Hela stayed to shake my hand.

"You did good," she said. "I know this was your first job with the Guild, and it was kind of a trial by fire, but you more than earned your share."

I grinned. "Does that mean I get a bigger share?"

She snorted. "Funny. Anyway, I'll tell Gavin you did good. Others will want to work with you, and I might hit you up myself next time I'm putting a crew together. Stay loose."

"Uh, you, too."

She nodded one final time at me, turned on her heel and moved back to the dock, where she slipped astride the back of a huge bat that looked like it had mange or something. I mean, it was a seriously ugly damn bat, and bats aren't exactly beauty queens to start with. It was kind of fitting, though. Not that Hela was ugly, but she was a goblin, and the sight of a goblin warrior riding a giant bat kind of worked. If she'd ridden a giant dove, I might have smirked, if you know what I mean.

I watched the direction she left by, then hopped aboard my own ride, my lovely, gleaming Chromecat. I stroked her curves (yes, I know how that sounds, but she was seriously strokeable), goosed her engine and took off into the skies, leaving that shady bar of ill repute behind.

I ducked into an alley, cloaked Chromecat and myself using my best spell, then sped off in the direction which Hela had vanished.

I prayed I wasn't too late.

Chapter 8

My heart stopped when I didn't see her. *Damn it all.* If she got away with Nevos's prize and delivered it to him, enabling him to do fuck all with it, and I'd *helped* her do it, I would never forgive myself. And it might bring hellacious harm to the world, too. I *had* to stop her.

I gasped with relief when I passed a building and saw her flying her bat down a cross-avenue. Narrowing my eyes, I turned Chromecat and followed. It occurred to me that I could dive-bomb her and waylay her, then steal the bag. On the other hand, I could let her lead me to Nevos. That made more sense to me.

It also posed more risk.

But no risk, no reward, right?

Hunching my back, praying I was making the right decision, I followed. Hela flew east, leaving the tall buildings of New York City behind and venturing over Long Island. Where the hell was she going? She flew on and on, and I began to worry about gas. Chromecat might be magical, but she still needed gas for her engine. I checked the gauge and was relieved—not even half empty. She used gas *slowly.* Thank goodness.

The homes below grew nicer, larger, more stately, and the grounds around them beautiful and well-manicured. The ocean stretched away to the right. I realized we were flying over the Hamptons and whistled to myself. It had been a long time since I'd made a visit to the Hamptons, and then it had only been because a guy I'd met in a bar promised to take me out on his yacht. Turns out *yacht* was a euphemism for *canoe*, and that was proportionally about right for other things regarding that jerkwad, too. Moving on.

Hela finally brought her bat lower to the ground. Unsurprisingly, cops on griffons rose to meet her. They fell in beside her, flanking her, and she exchanged a few words with them. Instead of driving her off, they escorted her on. Interesting. They must have been informed of her arrival.

They flew on, lowering toward the ground over Southampton. Frowning while simultaneously marveling at all the awesome mansions on display (seriously, the Hamptons rocked), I said a spell to reduce the noise of Chromecat's engine even more and trailed them. The griffon-mounted police brought Hela to one particular mansion along the beach, alighting in its driveway. A few security personnel came out to meet them, and the cops nodded and spoke to them, then took off.

I made a few circles of the mansion, heartened that no one seemed to notice me, then dipped down to the grounds and pulled Chromecat to a halt under some arching trees in the huge front lawn. A mansion by the beach in the Hamptons. Damn, Nevos sure knew how to live. And he'd only been in our world for a few months. Then again, maybe he was just visiting someone.

I killed the engine and climbed off, stretching to unkink the muscles of my shoulders and legs. That was the longest bike ride I'd ever been on. The thrill of flying for that long had put a grin on my face, but unfortunately it had also made my legs wobbly, and I stumbled a little as I pushed through the foliage toward the grand entrance of the mansion, where the guards were leading Hela.

A majordomo took over for them at the door, and they bowed and slunk away, disappearing into the shadows with supernatural skill. I realized they had magic on their side, too. Hopefully mine was better. I kept a close watch out for them as I made my way through the grounds, using all my skills as a thief and a semi-witch. Reaching a vine-covered brick wall, I climbed it to a window. Sensing heavy wards, I moved to the next window, then the next. All warded powerfully. *Damn.* I'd have to use some of my expensive new spellgredients to get through.

Swearing under my breath at the necessity, I mixed a potion and said a spell, carving a hole through the wards of a second story window, then opened it six inches. I peered in. A maid was walking away from me down the hall. I waited for her to disappear, then climbed through and dropped to the carpeted floor.

Where had Hela gone?

Hardly daring to breathe, I kept to the walls and shadows as I crept through the corridors of the mansion, making my way toward where I thought the majordomo was taking Hela. Sure enough, I arrived just as he was showing her to the top of a set of grand stairs and then along a high, clean, immaculate hall. Everything gleamed of crystal or gold. Pictures of yachts and sailboats hung on the walls.

I snuck up behind Hela and the majordomo.

This is it. Once I do this, there's no going back.

I snatched a gleaming gold candlestick off a passing table, rose and whacked the majordomo over the head. He crumpled to the floor without a sound. Even as Hela spun, I struck her, too, praying that my spells of darkness and stealth had prevented her from seeing my face. She grunted and collapsed.

I bent down, found the surprisingly small black velvet bag containing the mystery item, untied it from her belt and tied it to my own, then stood. I put my ear to a nearby door and listened. Hearing nothing on the other side, I opened the door, then dragged first the majordomo, then Hela inside. That should keep them out of sight until I was done.

Done with *what?* I thought as I closed the door on them.

Well, I had to make sure Nevos was here. Do that and I would get clear and summon the Fae Knights to take him down.

Pleased with my plan, I moved down the corridor toward its end. That had to be where the majordomo had been taking Hela.

My heart had been pounding so loudly in my ears that I hadn't even heard the music, but as I inched closer to the end of the hall it began to wash over me, and I blinked in surprise. What was that instrument? At first I couldn't place it, then realized it was violin music. Someone was playing the violin. The rich, complex sounds poured over me, lifting me up, dashing me down, spinning me around in a thousand directions. I was breathless with the beauty of it.

What the hell?

Wonderingly, I reached the end of the corridor and paused before a large oaken door with a sparkling brass knob. The music came from behind it. Nevos must be there. Somehow I just knew it.

My belly fluttered with nerves, and a thrill coursed down my spine as I lifted my hand to knock. I paused. Was knocking really the thing to do in a situation like this? Hela would have been admitted by the majordomo, but would he have knocked? Probably, I thought. How was I going to explain the absence of the majordomo? I would have to improvise.

I swallowed past the lump and my throat, then knocked.

The door, without me or anyone else touching it, swung open. I gasped at seeing what lay on the other side.

A gorgeous and half-naked Fae Lord played a violin with intense concentration, leaping on long, nimble legs from the carpeted floor to a sort of dais or stage, then spinning about to his audience, which was composed of two more Fae with more clothes on, one male and one female. I knew they were Fae instantly from their grace and power—I could sense it from where I stood. The man with the violin played on. Long, dark hair framed his eerily familiar face, and instantly I knew this was Nevos. He resembled Davril closely with his strong jaw and chiseled cheekbones, but his face was a bit leaner, more artistic, and his hair was long, shadowy and flowing over broad, naked shoulders. Clear sweat glistened on his hairless pecs and trickled down over his taut abs. He had broad shoulders that tapered down to a lean, narrow waist, and long graceful legs clad in black silk pants. His feet were bare.

He didn't stop playing when I opened the door. Eyes still closed, he sawed harder. Strange colors floated in the space around him, and belatedly I realized this was magic created from his music. His audience of two gasped appreciatively. He danced and pirouetted, clean sweat flying.

I stared, transfixed, my belly going flip-flop. Man, he looked so much like Davril! But so different, too. I didn't know what I had expected—some hideous monster, maybe—but it wasn't this.

At last he finished playing. Breathing heavily, he bowed to his audience, and they nodded their heads back to him. They didn't clap, they nodded. Maybe Fae didn't clap, I couldn't remember. I could barely remember my own name.

Nevos unfolded and turned to me. For the first time I saw his eyes. My core turned molten as those crystal green orbs pierced me.

"Yes?" he said, his voice smooth and deep. He didn't comment on my cat burglar outfit or the fact that I didn't look like one of his staff.

Get a grip, Jade.

Sucking it up, I stepped over the threshold and what must be a modified bedroom or playroom, occupied by lovely couches and expensive art. I patted the small velvet bag at my side.

"I have what you wanted," I said, speaking past the lump in my throat. I cast a glance at the other Fae, not sure how much I should reveal.

"You can speak openly," Nevos said.

Of course. These must be the two Fae that had come with him through the portal. They were his staunch loyalists, who had allowed themselves to be suspended in time and transported to another dimension in order to serve him. They watched me with curious but inscrutable expressions.

"I have the item stolen from the zeppelin," I said.

He nodded and stepped toward me. I had the urge to shrink away but managed to stand my ground. When he neared, my inner dragon stirred restlessly at his smell of sweat and power. Those brilliant green eyes drank me in, almost drowning me. I wanted to look away even more than I'd wanted to pull back, but I made myself return his gaze.

His eyes raked me up and down, and I shifted in discomfort.

"I'd expected a goblin," he said. One side of his mouth lifted. "I work with goblins quite a bit, and I would venture to say that you are not one."

My mouth was very dry. "I ... you can call me Jade." I wondered if he could see past my glamour. Those wizard guards could see through Lux's shadow-spell, so maybe they'd been able to see through my glamour, too. If they could, I wouldn't be surprised if Nevos could, too. Not that it mattered. He wouldn't have recognized me anyway. I'd only seen him for the merest instant the night of the stadium battle, and I hadn't recognized him.

"You can call me Nevos," he said. Bowing to me, he seemed to be waiting for something.

Feeling like a dolt, I realized what it was. I lifted my hand to him. Fluidly, he grasped it firmly but lightly at the same time, brought it to his lips and kissed it. His lips were hot and soft, and very full and kissable. He grinned at me as he kissed me, and my belly squirmed. I wished it would quit doing that.

I cast an annoyed glance at the other two Fae. Nevos was obviously powerful, and I was going to have my hands full (*Watch it, Jade*) dealing with him, let alone these other two. Somehow I needed to get rid of them, then subdue Nevos.

The impish part of me said, *Get him in bed and tie him up. Better tire him out first before I call in the Fae Knights.*

Down, girl!

"Well?" said Nevos, and I realized he must be staring at me. Had I zoned out? Sheesh!

The other two Fae were watching me with open amusement.

"Well what?" I said, annoyed.

Nevos's eyes flicked to the velvet bag. "I believe you came here to give me something."

"Oh. Right." My hand went to the bag. Paused. "I came here to sell you something, actually."

"Gavin assured me that all payment went through him."

"Oh. Yeah. That. Never mind."

He studied me. "Where is Hela? Also, why are you unaccompanied?"

"Er … your majordomo gave me the creeps. I told him I could find you on my own."

"Interesting …"

"And Hela got sick."

"Right after the burglary?" he said.

"Uh, I guess. That happens sometimes. Some people can't take the stress and get the squirts." My cheeks burned. "I mean, they get sick."

The other two Fae tittered. I was beginning to hate those assholes.

Nevos visibly shook it off. "Well, if that will be all, Mistress Jade, I believe I will take that now."

No putting this off anymore. Slowly I reached to the bag, unclipped it, then lifted it toward him. "It's on the inside," I said.

"I figured."

"I mean, the bag is magical. There's more space on the inside than it looks."

"I had assumed so."

Man, I was really botching this. And I was no closer to subduing Nevos or the dynamic duo. Oh well, that had only been Plan A. Plan B was to get the hell out of here now that I knew where he was and summon the cavalry. But was this place really his? How long would he stay here? I had a lot of questions. Unfortunately now wasn't the time to ask them.

But I really hated to leave him with that bag. He'd come to our world to take it over for his Master, and he needed whatever was in that bag to do it. Not only had I helped him get it, *but I'd brought it to him.* The very idea made me nauseous.

"Actually," I said, "there's more stuff in that bag. At least I think so."

"You don't remember putting it in there?"

"It's been a long week. Besides, that bag's valuable, and giving it over wasn't in the price Gavin and I agreed on." I snatched the bag back, and Nevos arched his eyebrows.

"Very well," he said. "Then shall we simply extract the item from the bag?"

"Er …"

Before I could clumsily begin doing this, a senior-looking guard in a nice suit burst into the room, his face red.

"My lord!" he said, and gave a hasty bow. "There's something you should see! Quickly!"

He ran past us, then the other two Fae, reached the balcony door and flung it open. Rushing onto the balcony, he stared up at something, then swore loudly. Gesturing back to us, he said, "Well?"

Such was the desperation on his face that we all emerged onto the balcony. A hot wind was blowing from somewhere, and I smelled fire. Then I glanced up to where the guard was pointing. Instantly I felt all the blood drain from my face, and my legs turned to rubber, but this time not from a long ride.

Above us, barreling toward the mansion with smoke trailing from its scaly mouth, was a dragon.

Chapter 9

"Holy shit," I said. "It's *him*."

Indeed, it was my arch-nemesis, Vincent Walsh, the owner of whatever was in the velvet bag that was bigger on the inside that the outside, and he looked *pissed*. His dragon form was not his usual shape, but it was impressive, huge and red, with wide batlike wings and ridges running down from his horned head all the way to his spiky tail.

"You know him?" Nevos asked me. He'd dropped his violin somewhere on the way to the balcony.

I patted the bag. "He's the owner of this."

Nevos's jaw bulged. "Walsh."

"Right."

As we watched, several police officers on griffons, aided by several police witches and wizards, were flying up to greet the dragon. Magical blasts sizzled out from police-issue wands, and red lightning leapt from the hands of a witch in a dark blue uniform. Vincent Walsh drove on through, rage boiling off him, and the police scattered to get out of his way.

"Can you hold him off?" I asked Nevos.

"Not from here. This is just a rental."

He whistled, then nodded to the other two Fae. Nodding back, they whistled loudly. Moments later three large winged forms swept in out of the darkness. Maybe they'd been on the roof or somewhere, I didn't know, but suddenly I was watching three dinosaur-like creatures flapping their wings in a holding position right below the balcony.

"Pterodactyls?" I said, feigning astonishment. Okay, I only had to fake it a little. I'd seen Nevos riding one during the battle of the mirror, but that had been a distant look, not an up-close-and-personal viewing like this. I could see the little hairs sticking out from the leathery skin of the beasts, and the mucous in their huge eyes.

"Tarons," Nevos corrected me. So saying, he leapt into the saddle of the central creature, and his two compatriots jumped into the saddles of theirs. To the guard, Nevos said, "Get clear and tell all the troops to pull back. We'll draw the worm away and contact you later."

"Do you think it will follow?" the guard said. His face was tight as a drum.

Nevos held up a palm. The velvet bag ripped out of my hand and flew into his.

"Hey!" I said.

"He's after this," Nevos told the guard. "He must be able to sense it. That's how he found us. He'll follow me to get it back, I'm sure of it."

"Thank you, sir."

I was impressed. Nevos wasn't a coward, and he wasn't going to use his men to shield him from the oncoming doom. He would shield *them*, even use himself as bait to draw Walsh away. Traitor and evil though he may have been, he was downright heroic in his own way.

Just the same, I swore. Walsh had done much the same thing to me—that is, using telekinesis to rip a prized object from my possession. Well, I wasn't going to take it this time. I whistled, too, and in seconds Chromecat screamed out of the darkness, engines throbbing, feathery black wings pumping.

Walsh was very close now. In seconds he would be near enough to set the mansion on fire.

I jumped astride Chromecat and glared at Nevos. "I'm not leaving your side until I get that bag back," I said. "Either that or you pay me for it!"

Eyes flinty, he jerked the reins of his taron and flew it up into the night. His riders flanked him. Pressing my thighs into Chromecat's sighs, and praying I was making the right decision, I followed. The mansion receded below, and the cold winds of night enfolded me, streaming my hair out behind me. I said a spell to lessen the effects of the wind and glanced behind us.

Walsh had veered away from the mansion, just like Nevos had predicted. Unfortunately, he was streaking right for us. Again, just like Nevos had said. I'd been pursued once by Walsh in dragon form, and that hadn't gone well at all. It had taken the Queen of the Fae herself to drive the bastard off. Nevos was obviously powerful and brave, but how could he defeat the likes of Vincent Walsh?

Walsh drove on, fire licking his lips. One of the Fae riders turned back to blast him with a bolt of light from his palm. The light struck Walsh on one of his horns and bounced off.

The other rider tried, then Nevos. Nothing.

Walsh was upon us. The four of us circled him, blasting him with beams of energy and the various spells we could conjure. I hit him with a freezing blast and a broiling wind, but he didn't even seem to feel them. A dozen policemen and –women swirled around him, too. We must have been a hell of a sight, all of us aerial magic-users sweeping and dodging the snapping jaws and plumes of fire of that great primordial, almost elemental beast as he tore through the skies, smoke issuing from his nostrils, eyes flashing with hate. It felt weird to be fighting alongside both the police *and* Nevos, who was the enemy of mankind, as far as I could tell, against Walsh, but life is weird that way.

At last Walsh broke away from us, scattering us with his wings and fire, then flying a short distance away, wheeling about, and driving straight at us again. Fire erupted from his mouth in a long, bright column, aimed right at the center of our numbers. Desperately we flew out of the way, each going in a separate direction.

Realizing that force couldn't defeat Walsh, Nevos said, "To me!" and flew west. His two riders fell in behind him.

"Not without me!" I said.

Gunning Chromecat, I raced to catch up with him. Nevos threw me an annoyed look but didn't dispute the issue.

I heard the crackle of fire. Glancing back, I saw a spear of flame racing toward me. Suppressing a scream, I jerked the handlebars, veering to the right. I felt the heat of the flames as they whoosed past. Eyes wide, I rejoined the others, who all looked just as grim as I felt.

"We've got to get rid of him," said one of the riders, the male one. I wondered if they were renegade Fae Knights like those that served Prince Jereth.

"I have an idea," called the female rider. Concentrating, she gestured at the bag Nevos had strapped to his belt. He was still shirtless and barefooted. He was an amazing sight, bare-chested and dashingly handsome, riding that dinosaur while a dragon chased him. As the female rider worked her magic, a magical glow emanated from the bag and flew into her hands. Then another glow materialized and flew into the hands of the other rider. They were replicas of the velvet bag.

"Well done!" said Nevos. "But are you sure?"

"We'll do what we can, my lord."

She jerked the reins of her taron and veered to the right. The male rider jerked the reins of his and veered to the left.

Behind us Walsh roared in anger. I glanced over my shoulder to see him pursue the male rider.

Coming alongside Nevos, I said, "What just happened?"

"Lyra made a copy of the magical signature of the item," Nevos said. "Two copies. She took one and Tae took the other. Now Walsh doesn't know who has what he's looking for."

I whistled. "Lyra and Tae might have gotten themselves killed."

"No. The magical construct will only exist for a few minutes. When it dissipates, he'll come back after us. After me," he corrected himself. He frowned. "Can you please leave now? You're safe to go."

I made my voice firm. "I still don't have my bag back."

He let out a sigh. "Very well. Ra!"

He gave his ride his heels and it shot forward. I was amazed by how fast the creature could go. Then again, it was no mere animal, I knew. Like Chromecat and Lady Kay, it was magically augmented.

"Where are we going?" I said.

"You mean where am *I* going?"

"Whatever. Back to the mansion?"

"No, I must get somewhere secure. There's only one place I know to escape a dragon of that power. Luckily, it's the place I would have been headed to anyway. It's where I have to go to use this." He batted the velvet bag. Just what was *in* there? And why did Walsh and Nevos need the same thing?

"Too bad," I said. "I liked that place." The truth was I was very happy not to go back to the mansion in the

Hamptons. Hela would be waking up soon, and I didn't want her to know it had been me that clocked her.

Still, I allowed myself to feel a pang at missed opportunities as I turned back to see the Hamptons begin to recede behind me. *Someday*, I thought. *Someday I'll come back here and explore you more thoroughly.* I would get onboard a yacht someday if it killed me.

I turned back around. The skyscrapers of New York City drew closer. We were returning home. But where could we be headed that would stand up to a dragon? Where would a dragon not want to enter?

Shit.

"Not *there*," I muttered. I thought I knew where we were going.

Damn it all, why does it have to be THERE?

Manhattan approached, maddeningly swiftly. Were we traveling faster than before? It sure as hell seemed like it. It was always the places you wanted to go to least that you headed to fastest. Some sort of natural law, I guess.

As we went, I traded sidelong glances with Nevos. Or at least I studied him out of the corner of my eye, and I could sense him studying me out of the corner of his. Fuck, but Davril had one hot brother. I mean, he wasn't hotter than Davril, that would be hard, but he did the Stormguard name proud, I can tell you that. A shame he was evil.

Maybe he's not, I thought. *Maybe it was all a hilarious misunderstanding.* I could taste the hilarity on my lips.

No, that was bugs. I renewed the spell that kept out wind and bugs.

Spitting occasionally, I kept looking over my shoulder to see if Vincent Walsh had found us yet. Sure enough, just as we were passing over the first spires of New York City, a monstrous winged form slipped down out of the clouds above, fire licking at its lips.

"Walsh!" I said, unconsciously driving closer to Nevos.

He grinned at me. "I'll protect you."

"Hey!" Cheeks burning, I drove further away. Damned if I'd be protected from scorching, burning dragonfire by the likes of him!

I looked in my rearview. Fire was building up in the back of Walsh's throat.

"He's preparing another blast," I said, and started to split away from him so that we could divide around it.

"Hold on, Jade. Like I told you, I've got this."

Before I could decide if he was being serious or not, Walsh breathed out a terrible column of fire. It raced toward us faster than I'd expected. If I hadn't hesitated due to Nevos's claim, I could have evaded it, but as it was I was toast. Unless …

Eyes hard, Nevos took one hand off the reins of his taron and held it out behind him. A great orange energy exploded out from it, becoming a half-sphere of brilliant light. The dragonfire struck it. Some of the fire rebounded, some was absorbed and the rest deflected off of it.

"Wow!" I said, genuinely impressed. "That's some shield!"

He lifted a cocky eyebrow. "Like I said."

I drifted closer to him—unconsciously, I swear. Sheesh! I'm no slut. Not that I'm slut shaming. Okay, the truth is I'm totally a slut. Live it, learn it, love it. But I wasn't going to start a thing with Nevos, of all people. Davril would never let me hear the end of it.

"Okay, what next?" I said. "Can you protect us from every blast?"

He grimaced. "No. We've got to get to cover."

I flew down toward the city. We put a skyscraper between us and Walsh, then another. And another. He hunted us from above, smoke wreathing his scaly head, but he couldn't get at us, at least for a moment, and he knew it. Worse for him, the cops of the city had taken notice. They swarmed him in greater numbers than those of the Hamptons, and with better magic, too. Nevos and I had a chance to think.

"Well?" I said.

"Do you have any ideas?"

"Well, flying is his element, unless you think we can beat him … wherever we're going?" I was all too aware of where that must be. When Nevos shook his head, I said, "Then I guess we hit the streets."

With obvious reluctance, Nevos nodded.

We descended from the skies and alit on the sidewalk. Passersby stared at us, then hastily found other places to be when Nevos's dinosaur snapped its long sharp beak in their direction.

"You can't ride that thing down the street," I said.

"I don't intend to."

Nevos whispered in the ear hole of the taron. It pumped its wings and lifted off, vanishing around a tall building.

"He'll meet us at our destination, along with my compatriots," Nevos said. "Walsh won't follow him. He'll follow us. This." Again he patted the velvet bag.

We'd landed on the street, and the drivers behind us were overcoming their fear to start honking. I indicated the seat behind me and said, "Get on."

Nevos did, and I could feel his hard eight-pack against the small of my back and his powerful arms wrapping around me.

"Er, invasion of privacy?" I said, but I didn't fight it too hard. I gunned the motor and shot Chromecat forward. She tucked in her black wings, becoming a street vehicle once more, and in seconds we were virtually indistinguishable from the rest of the traffic.

Glancing overhead from time to time, I could still see Walsh hunting us through the skies, shooting flame at the cops who harassed him and sending them scurrying. He might not be able to see us anymore, but I was sure he could still sense the item in the bag. I only prayed that it wasn't as important to him as the golden antler had been. Hopefully he'd just absorbed too much dragon over the years and had become a … wait for it … hoarder. Har har.

Because if the item in the bag were important to him … Well, last time he'd kidnapped my sister. I wasn't looking forward to what he might do in the next go round.

"Where are we going?" I said, darting between two cars. Horns honked, but I didn't care. I didn't have time to sit and wait to get roasted. And it was better for them, too, even if they didn't know it.

"Turn right," Nevos said. Then, a few blocks later: "Left."

He continued giving directions, never telling me where our ultimate destination was, but the looming shadow of Central Park continued to get larger in my field of vision with every heartbeat, and a sense of dread certainty settled over me.

"Just spit it out," I said finally. "We're going there, aren't we?" I pointed at the shadow that was the mystical veil surrounding what had once been a bright green spot in a sea of steel and concrete.

"That's right," Nevos said, sounding pleased. "So you see, we must part ways when we get to the barrier. You wouldn't want to go across the Veil, would you?"

"Ha! You're not getting rid of me that easily, buster. I'm going across with you, like it or not."

"What about your bike? It can't go in. Or at least I don't think it would get very far."

"I can have her wait or circle. You let me worry about Chromecat."

"Chromecat?" He tasted the word. "Nice."

A thrill ran through me. *See, I KNEW it was a good name!* Then again, was Nevos really the arbiter of taste? I thought of him playing his violin half-naked and had to concede that he might just be.

I slowed as we reached the area around Central Park. There were the usual half-broken walls and barricades, and a police zeppelin was sweeping the skies overhead—too far away to see us, but it was coming in our direction. It wasn't illegal to go into the park, but I didn't want to draw attention, either.

Beyond the barricades rose the misty gray Veil itself, what looked like a weird cloud permanently camped out over Central Park, completely sealing it off. It rose into an irregular dome a few hundred feet high. No one could see into the park from outside, at least no one I knew, and what went on in there was largely a mystery. I'd been in there, of course, and knew that it was much bigger on the inside than the out, and that it was populated by monsters, outlaws and monster outlaws. Along with other, stranger things.

Nevos and I hopped off Chromecat. I whispered to her, and she took off, gorgeous black wings flapping. I knew she would be ready when I needed her again, but it pained me to be apart from her. I really did love my ride.

Nevos watched me watching Chromecat, but when I turned to him he didn't comment on it. Wearing a small smile, he bowed and gestured to the Veil.

"After you," he said.

Amazing, I thought. He was so much smoother and less rigid than Davril. He had just arrived in this world and he acted as if he'd been here for years. With Davril it was the opposite. It occurred to me that I could learn more about Davril hanging out with Nevos than I could with Davril himself.

I started to reply, but just then a titanic roar made my head snap up.

Walsh had just emerged from around a skyscraper. Fire flicking in the back of his maw, he barreled down at us.

"Shit!" I said. "He's seen us!"

"Hurry," Nevos said.

He moved toward the barricade, and I went with him. We found a crack in the half-ruined structure and passed through it, then approached the Veil itself. Misty currents stirred in the unnatural cloud, completely independent from the wind.

"Here goes nothing," I muttered.

Walsh roared again. Flame leapt from his mouth, streaking right at us. As one, Nevos and I ran forward, into the mist. Instantly Walsh's roars faded from hearing, and I was pretty sure his fire would simply bounce off the Veil. It was impenetrable to most magic. Just to be sure, though, I kept running.

We threaded our way through dense trees and dangled undergrowth. The park had once been stately and orderly, but now it was a vast, sprawling forest. No more roars came, and the trees didn't burst into flames behind us. My heart thumped wildly, and sweat stuck my clothes to the small of my back.

Gasping, I drew to a stop.

Nevos stopped, too, and turned to me. Sweat gleamed on his bare chest. Inside the Veil we could see sky, but it was nighttime. It was always nighttime here. Fortunately the full moon shone down, giving us some illumination, and my shifter senses could see well in the dark. I was sure Nevos could, too. After all, his brother was able to.

"That was close," Nevos said, his muscular chest rising and falling.

"Yeah." I doubled over and clutched my knees. "Think Walsh will come after us?"

"I doubt it. We're in Shadowpark, now. That's what they call it in here."

"Oh?"

"There's a reason people don't come in here," Nevos said. "Hopefully that deterrent extends to dragons. But if it doesn't, that's fine, too. I have allies here."

"Allies that can ward off Vincent Walsh?"

"Even him. Come. Let's—"

He broke off as new sounds reached us. The small hairs along my arms lifted. What was this? The sounds were soft but clear, as of a number of people or beings moving in a coordinated way through the forest. And there was an odor, a strange acrid odor … strangely familiar …

Nevos realized it first.

"Goblins!" he whispered, careful to keep his voice low. "It's a band of goblins."

Chapter 10

I tasted bile in the back of my throat.

"Goblins?" I said. "Are you sure?"

Taking my hand, he guided me through the undergrowth, then crouched down. I followed suit, and together we peered through the brush as a war-like band of humanoid figures with green skin, claws and tusks moved through the forest. They went with stealth and speed, making very little noise. If Nevos and I hadn't been supernaturally gifted, we probably wouldn't have been able to hear them. I guessed there were about twenty or twenty-five of them.

And they were coming our way.

"Damn it all," I said.

Nevos peered upward, as if looking for something, then nodded, as if to confirm his suspicions, and pointed. I looked and saw a shape hunched on a branch overhead. Tusks gleamed faintly on the figure's head.

"Goblin bands always send out scouts," Nevos said.

You would know. "Maybe they're friendly?"

The goblin scout in the trees cupped his hands to his mouth and hooted like an owl. An answering howl came from the band even then moving toward us. There must have been a code hidden in the hoot because the scout, upon hearing it, pulled something that had been hanging from his belt and shook it out. As he did, it expanded—a weighted net.

He threw it down at us.

Nevos and I jumped in opposite directions. The net spread, catching on the bushes where we'd just been, and when I glanced up the goblin scout had vanished. I heard a hoot, I wasn't sure from where, but I knew it was probably informing the goblin band that we were still free.

As in answer, the members of the goblin band picked up speed.

Nevos and I looked at each other. I knew my face must be pale and tight. Every muscle in my body had tensed.

"Run," he said.

He picked himself up and darted through the forest. Breathless, I followed. A whistling sound reached my ears, and I dodged to the side just as a spear hurtled through the space where my head had just been. It struck a tree and imbedded itself six inches in the wood. *That could've been me!*

"Why are they hunting us?" I said between breaths. I wanted to add *Aren't they your allies?* but held myself back.

"Who knows," he said over his shoulder. "They're goblins!"

"That's racist!"

Another whistling sound reached me. I flinched to the left, and the spear flashed by, aimed straight for the small of Nevos's back. He spun, amazingly fast, and knocked it aside with his hand.

"Wow," I said, genuinely impressed.

He didn't acknowledge the compliment but ran on. Evidently he didn't trust in his skill to keep doing that.

Breathless, branches and undergrowth whipping at us, we fled through the dark forest as the goblins chased us. Spears flew, but we dodged them with gasps and swears. I was beginning to run out of breath when Nevos pointed and said, "There!"

I saw a dark opening in a low rise. Nevos threw himself into it. I followed him into the cave, wishing there was some alternative. But it was either that or get caught by the goblins, and they didn't seem like they were in the mood to make friends. Side by side in the tight space, Nevos and I waited, watching and listening for the approach of the goblin band.

"They're going to see us," I whispered.

He frowned. His eyes fell on a boulder not far away. Lifting his palm toward it, he made the boulder levitate and float through the air toward us.

"Oh my God," I breathed. "You're using the Force!"

"Pardon?"

I didn't explain, and it didn't matter. He brought the boulder before the entrance to the cave, then set it down, sealing us in darkness with each other. I could feel his breaths against my skin and the heat of his skin. Distantly through the stone filtered the sounds of the goblins approaching. They grunted and hooted, seeming to mill about, but they couldn't find us.

They didn't go away, though.

"Damn, they can track us," I said. "They'll know we didn't go any further. Unless you have some magic for that, too."

"Unfortunately, no. We'd better see where this cave goes."

I did have a spell for magical illumination. Ruby had taught it to me. I said the words, and a blob of blue light leapt from my palm. I could see well in places where there was little light, but I couldn't see jack without *some* light. Leading the way, I left the entrance of the cave behind and followed the corridor as it sloped subtly downward. I'd expected it to end shortly, but it kept going. I hit a branch and took the right-hand path. Everything stank of mud and stone and minerals. Somewhere water dripped.

"Can you hear the goblins anymore?" I said.

"No, can you?"

"No."

"That's something, at least."

"Yeah," I said. "And I don't think Walsh followed us past the Veil."

"Let's hope not. We've got enough problems, don't we?"

I let myself smile, just a little. "I guess you could say that. Hey, it's all a day's work for a thief in modern New York City. I admit the goblins were a surprise, though. I knew there were a few of them around, here and there, but in these numbers?"

"I didn't know of it, either." The idea seemed to bother him, and I wondered what it meant. He and the goblins both served the Shadow, right? Maybe this was an example of the right hand and the left working separately.

"This stupid cave better go somewhere," I said, trying and failing to peer ahead.

"It does. I can smell fresh air coming from ahead. It's faint, though."

"You have a good nose. I don't smell anything."

"You're part shifter, aren't you?" he said.

"How did you know?"

"You're too fast, for one. And I'm sure your sense of smell is stronger than a human's, too."

"My strong is also stronger," I quipped.

"Cute."

"I try."

Shit, was I *flirting* with him? He was the enemy! I concentrated on remembering why that was. He had betrayed Davril. He had sided with the Shadow and opened the very gates of Stormguard Castle, allowing a wave of goblins to pour in. That had begun the final war between the Fae and the agents of the Shadow, and ultimately the Shadow had prevailed and the Fae Lords had fled their homeworld entirely. All because of Nevos. *Remember that, Jadeslut.*

But it was hard, especially when I turned to catch him watching my ass. His eyes flicked up, but too late. I'd seen the direction of his gaze. And *my* gaze lingered, just a little too long, on his taut, lithe, muscular chest. I forgot what I was about to say. Cheeks burning, I turned back around.

Well, that had been awkward.

He cleared his throat. "Um …"

"Yes?" I said hopefully, eager to have something else to focus on.

Then: "Never mind."

I sighed. Yep. Pretty awkward.

Finally, lamely, he said, "So you're a thief, then?"

It was a pathetic stab at conversation, but I seized on it. "That's right," I said. "And a half-shifter. And I can make a mean martini, too." *Stop flirting, Jadeslut!*

"What do you shift into? Or half-shift?"

"Well, nothing now. Long story. But I used to be able to partially shift into a dragon."

He made a sound of appreciation. "A dragon! That's interesting. But how do you half shift into a dragon?"

"Basically, just the wings. Oh, and being able to breathe fire."

"So you could fly?"

I nodded sadly, watching my blue light flicker along the wet stone hall. "That's right. It was awesome. But I can't do it anymore." *Thanks to Walsh, the bastard.* "I don't want to talk about that. Enough about me. Since we're stuck together for the moment, maybe you can tell me about yourself." *Please please please. And don't skimp on the Davril dishing, either.*

"I don't want to talk about that," he said. "If you'll forgive me. Employer-employee privilege, I hope you understand."

"Top secret stuff, huh?"

"If you like."

He didn't add anything to that, and I wondered how far I could press him before he caught on to my ulterior motives.

"But it must be some big thing to steal from a dragon mage," I said.

"Evidently." At first that was all he would say about it, and I slumped, but then he added, "It's only the first stage, though. There's something more I need."

My ears perked up. "Oh?"

"Something that will help me complete my goals."

"What are your goals?"

There was a smile in his voice as he said, "That would be telling."

Indeed it would. But would that be so wrong? I could use a little telling, right about now. But I guessed I would have to wait. Part of me wanted to spin around, grab a rock and hit him over the head. Then I could tie him up and steal the velvet bag. That was my mission, right? But I knew he was too fast, too strong and too powerful. I couldn't defeat him on my own, and trying would only give the game away and probably get me killed.

A smell hit me. I sniffed.

"I sense it, too," I said. "Fresh air."

I quickened my pace. We rounded one bend, then another. The light grew stronger, at last growing bright enough for me to douse my magical fire, which was good because it was about out of mojo anyway. Finally we emerged under the moonlight once more, still under the canopy of the endless trees of Shadowpark. Some of the trees looked sinister, with weird boles and roots grasping like tentacles, but others were stately and handsome specimens that made me long for primordial times. I was beginning to feel like I was stuck in a Tarzan and Jade novel, only with a Tarzan that had gone bad.

But he looked oh so good.

"I hear something," I said.

Crouching, we moved into a copse of trees. There were noises ahead—the tread of several sets of moving feet creeping softly through the forest.

"Better not be more damned goblins," I said.

"I don't think so," Nevos said.

Or werewolves, I added to myself. The alpha of the pack 'round these parts probably wouldn't be so happy to see me, either.

Surprisingly, Nevos smiled and stood. "Boys," he said. "I've been looking for you."

He stepped forward, out from the cover of the trees and onto a narrow path. The people we'd been hiding from turned out to be half a dozen biker-types, wearing lots of leather and sporting copious ink. All were male except one, and she was as big and mean-looking as any of the fellas.

I instantly recognized their ilk as those who worked for Angela. *Damn it*, I thought. *I get tired of being right*. Nevos had come here to make contact with the witch herself. And it wasn't just to seek her protection against Walsh, I now knew. It had something to do with the item I'd helped steal. That I'd *turned over* to Nevos.

Davril had been right. I did have a game.

But my game really, really sucked.

Hoping I could right the wrongs I'd caused, I made myself step forward and join Nevos. The biker-types didn't even lift an eyebrow.

"Good to see you again, my lord," said the burliest of the bikers, a guy with a big bushy beard shot through with gray. The words *my lord* sounded strange coming from someone like him, but he said them smoothly enough. Angela had them well trained.

"You know these guys?" I asked Nevos, playing my part.

"They work for … a friend of mine," he said. I thought he'd been about to say *They work for me*, but maybe not. But if he *had*, that was really interesting. Did some of Angela's goons serve both her *and* Nevos? Or *just* Nevos? Did *my lord* mean more than it had sounded?

"Shall we escort you out of the Veil or to the Mistress?" asked Graybeard. "Or somewhere else entirely?"

"They're very accommodating," I said.

Still wearing that small smile, Nevos said, "To the Mistress, please." To me, he said, "Are you sure you still wish to accompany me? I can have Maggie here take you out of Shadowpark, and you can be on your way. I'll send you the bag later via Gavin, or payment if you prefer."

"Nope. I'm sticking with you. And my bag."

"Suit yourself. But it may be dangerous where we're going."

I snorted. "We were just chased by a dragon, then a band of goblins. I can deal with a biker rally."

The bikers grinned at each other.

"Cute," said one, and I didn't know if he meant me or my comment. Either way, I didn't fear being recognized. The glamour that had hidden my identity so far would hopefully go on doing so. Like the magical fire, I knew it couldn't go on forever, but it would last me longer than the fire had. Hopefully for long enough to get clear of this place and get back to Davril. Er, I meant the Fae.

Davril was just my partner.

For a moment, I allowed myself to wonder where he was and what he was doing. I missed his presence. Especially when I was out having misadventures in Shadow-freaking-park. Blech!

"Well, shall we?" Nevos asked me.

He ushered me into the heart of the goon squad, Graybeard snapped an order, and the whole troop got under way. Graybeard, whose name turned out to be Manx (because of course it was), informed us that his group was just performing routine patrols when they'd come across a creepy scene: human skulls on stakes, arranged in a complicated shape, with unknown characters painted on the skulls.

"Must be the goblins," I said.

"Goblins?" Manx said, as we went along.

"We just came across a band of them," Nevos agreed. "They could be responsible for the site. It sounds like some sort of ritual magic. Goblins have all sorts of dark rites. I would have to see the characters painted on the skulls to know for sure."

We pushed deeper into the vast, haunted forest, and I glanced all around frequently. I didn't trust that the goblins were gone, or Walsh for that matter. We saw no sign of them, though. All too soon, lights blazed through the trees, and the sounds of many people and the smell of roasting meat hit us.

"Welcome to the home of Mistress Angela," Nevos said, as we arrived at the tall trees that housed Angela's camp. Lean-tos and huts sprouted from the higher reaches of the trees, and ramps and walkways spanned the gaps between thick trunks. Like before, I thought of an evil version of the Ewok village in *Return of the Jedi*, or at least a pirate version of it. "She's an ally of mine," Nevos added. "Be respectful to her and you'll be fine. Probably."

"You're real encouraging."

He rolled his shapely shoulders. "She's a touchy one. She's committed everything to the fight we're now engaged in, and recently she lost her daughter to it. It's made her even more on edge."

I hit a twinge of discomfort. I had killed Blackfeather, Angela's daughter. Actually, it would be more accurate to say that I'd been trying to kill Angela but that Blackfeather had thrown herself between my knife and her mother. In a way, she'd killed herself. But that didn't stop her from appearing in my dreams sometimes, and for guilt to rip at me whenever I thought of her, which was more often than I'd like.

"Should we come with you, my lord?" Manx asked. "Escort you to the Mistress?"

"That won't be necessary," Nevos said. "I can see myself there. Thank you for the company in getting here, though. I'll let you resume your patrol now, or perhaps you're ready to knock off for the evening."

"Not with those gobs out there doing gods-know-what," Manx said.

He led his gang back into the forest. Nevos and I turned our attention to the village in the trees. My mind drifted back to that fateful day on the crystal stairs.

Blackfeather hadn't been evil, after all. She'd served her mother, who *was* evil, and she definitely wasn't *good*, but in the end she'd sacrificed herself to save her mother's life. It was hard to hate someone like that, and easy to feel guilty about ending her life. Of course, if she'd been *truly* good she would just have let me do the deed, right? That's what I tried to tell myself.

"Jade?" Nevos asked.

I jerked myself out of the reverie. "Yeah?"

"You can stay here or come with me. If you come, you'll get to meet Angela."

This should be fun. But if I didn't go, I would be that much further from the secrets of the velvet bag.

"What are we waiting for?" I said.

Chapter 11

We marched up a ramp to the second story of the village, then found a ramp to the third. Taking a rope bridge, we crossed to another level, and another. Around us rough-looking men and women in leather and tattoos came and went from huts and halls. There were also plenty of witches and wizards, mages devoted to the dark arts who served Angela. *Damn, there's too many.* I'd hoped more had died in the battle of the stadium, or at least run away, forsaking their allegiance to Angela. To the Shadow. But nope. Maybe Nevos's arrival had rallied even more to her cause.

"What do you think?" Nevos asked as we went along.

"Not bad," I said. I was surprised by his wanting to make small talk at all. Davril rarely did.

Dark shadows fell across the bridge we were traveling on—shadows with wings. I jerked my head up to see several giant blackbirds sweep through the skies overhead, circle around a certain tower, then fly into it through an appropriately sized opening. It must be their roost.

"Don't mind them," Nevos said. "They're the Razor Wings. Shapechangers and witches, high in the councils of Mistress Angela. Friendly enough, if you're allied with the Mistress."

"Does that include me?" I batted my eyes at him, and he laughed. A warm flutter spread through my belly. *Bastard*, I thought. *Won't you at least put a shirt on? You're making this more difficult than it has to be.* My natural flirtometer was getting confused, and I couldn't shut it off.

"We'll see," he said. "We'll see."

A large structure appeared ahead, a multi-storied building sprouting from a huge redwood-like tree. Stained glass windows winked from between knotted boles oozing bitter-smelling sap. It wasn't the same structure Davril and I had broken into to save Federico, but it was about the same general size and altitude. Two grim witches in flowing black robes stood to either side of the door. Their eyes had been gouged out, and black pits gaped where they had been. Instead of revealing scar tissue and empty sockets, though, the pits plunged into an endless blackness like the void itself. They must be connected with some other plane. Their appearance made shivers course down my back.

Surprisingly, they bowed their heads as Nevos approached.

"Are you here to see Our Lady?" said one, her voice like the creaking of pines.

"I am. And I have a guest." Nevos indicated me.

Wordlessly, the two witches drew away from the door. It swung open without either touching it, revealing a dark interior. Goosebumps popped out on my arms. *Last chance to chicken out.*

With gentlemanly aplomb, Nevos placed a hand on the small of my back and gently guided me inside Angela's freaky treehouse. It smelled of incense and resin. At first all I saw were shadows, but then Nevos waved a hand and the surroundings snapped into focus: surprisingly homey-looking couches and chairs with tapestries hanging from the wooden walls.

A figure was just coming down the tight spiral staircase that led to both a lower and an upper level: Angela. I recognized her flowing black robes and bouncing auburn hair. Steeling myself, I tried to appear like someone who hadn't been responsible for her daughter's death and who didn't know what all this craziness was about.

Angela stepped off the stairs and approached us. She looked younger than last time, with freckles on her cheeks and a cute pert nose. Brown eyes gazed out at us from a deceptively pretty face. Obviously she used magic to lengthen her lifespan and delay aging, even reverse it. Who knew how old she really was? She could be hundreds of years old for all I knew. Then again, she could be using a glamour like I was. Maybe those cute freckles really hid crow's feet. There was no way to tell.

"Well well," she said, smiling at Nevos. "Good to see you again, my friend." Her eyes raked his naked torso. "So much of you."

He grinned. "Good to see you, as well." He grasped her hand and kissed it, just as he had mine, and she smiled, seeming to enjoy the attention. Was *that* why she'd altered her appearance? Did she ... *like* Nevos? The idea made my head spin. I don't know why, but it surprised me. I guess I just never thought of Angela as human enough to have crushes.

"And who is this?" Angela said, swinging her attention to me.

"This is Jade, or at least that's what she calls herself," Nevos said. "One of the thieves I hired to steal that certain item from the mage. You know thieves and names."

"Ah, yes. Of course. Well, Jade, if that's what you like to call yourself, you are welcome in my camp, and my home."

"Er, thank you," I managed. What next? Would we sit down for tea and crackers?

"It *is* interesting that you're here," she said, and waited for some explanation.

"The mage could sense the item," Nevos said. "He wanted it back and came after it. Jade and I were forced to flee together."

"He took the form of a dragon," I added.

"A sacred form," Angela said.

I tried to hide a frown. A *sacred* form? That was a weird thing to say.

Angela shook it away. "Well, was the venture successful, Nevos? Did you acquire it?"

He patted the velvet bag at his side. "It is, as they say here, in the bag."

"Excellent!" She visibly composed herself. "Can I see it?"

"Certainly."

Finally, I thought. I would get to see what all the fuss was about.

Nevos moved the bag into his palm and lifted it up, spreading its flap with the fingers of his free hand. He paused, then reached into it, feeling around … and around … just how much stuff was *in* there? … and finally pulling out …

I stared.

"What is that?" I said.

Nevos handed me the bag. Idly, I stuffed it into a pouch on my belt, but my attention was fixed on the thing in his palm. At first I thought it was a large wooden button, but then I realized it was, or at least it resembled, a wooden handle or knob, like the sort you'd use to open a drawer on a chest.

"It's a handle," Nevos said, obviously enjoying my confusion.

Angela stretched out her hand. "Give it here." When Nevos placed it on her palm, she stared at it avidly, then closed her eyes. I knew she must be communing with it, or getting some magical read on the thing. When she was finished, she opened her eyes and breathed out. "It's the one. This is it at last. Your work in the outside world was worth it."

Nevos bowed his head, accepting the praise. "Thank you. Of course, I couldn't have done it without my new friend."

Angela's voice turned brittle. "Then thank you, too. *Jade.*"

The distaste dripped from her word. "Yeah. Sure," I said. Hopefully I was a better actress than she was. "But what did I help with? What is it? A drawer knob? I don't get it."

"It's the door to a wardrobe," Nevos said.

"Well, that explains everything. I love wardrobes! I hope I get first crack at rifling through it."

"Not that kind of wardrobe, Jade."

"Oh, poo." I placed my hands on my hips and tried to look commanding. "Then *what* kind? Because Vincent Walsh may be a snappy dresser, but I don't think he'd go through that much trouble to snazz up his look."

"That's none of your business," Angela said.

I opened my mouth to argue, but Nevos added, "She's right, Jade. I'm sorry. I know you've gone to considerable trouble and peril, but you did take that upon yourself. The objective we seek is something outside the scope of your contract."

I stared from Nevos to the knob, then from the knob to Angela. She watched me, an unpleasant, knowing smirk on her face. I resisted the urge to stick my tongue out at her, but it was a near thing.

"A soldier is to do and die, huh?" I said. Off his blank look, I said, "Never mind." Guess they didn't read Tennyson in the Fae Lands.

Angela shoved the knob into a pocket. "I will have to perform a working on it," she said. "I'll start right away, but I don't expect to finish for some hours. You can get comfortable and enjoy yourself, Nevos. I'll contact you when it's done."

"Very well."

To me, she added, "I'm sure Nevos will see you out."

Piqued, I said, "That's it? After all that and you're kicking me out?"

Nevos smiled disarmingly at Angela. "My dear, let her stay. She's been through a lot, and she deserves a rest. I'm sure she's hungry, too. Let her stay tonight. I'll find her accommodations. Who knows, by tomorrow she could decide to join our cause."

Fat chance, I thought. But I nodded. "Sure. Sounds good. I am hungry."

Angela's eyes were cold. "Then so be it."

She turned on her heels and vanished up the stairs. I started to breathe a sigh of relief, then remembered she had the knob, *whatever* that meant, and that I'd been the one to provide it. *Real good job, Jade. Find out what the villains' plans are by helping them accomplish it!*

"Well?" said Nevos. "Shall we find something to eat?"

"I am starving," I admitted.

We left Angela's lair and moved along the ramps and walkways of the arboreal village. A vague wind stirred the leaves and ruffled my hair, but it felt good, and I leaned into it as we went. Nevos walked very close to me, and from time to time I got the impression he was tempted to place an arm around my waist or shoulders. If he had, I would've been tempted to let him. But he didn't, so I wasn't forced to decide. Yet.

The moment might be coming, I thought.

We found some biker types grilling meat on a projection of one of the walkways. Mugs of beer were shoved into our hands, then skewers of meat. We laughed and ate, then drank. Neither of us spoke, but that was okay. It was surprisingly easy to share this moment with Nevos. With Davril, it was often awkward. He was so courtly, mannered and reserved. Nevos was relaxed. Wild. And, I have to admit, I was a bit wild myself.

He's evil, I reminded myself for the hundredth time. *Eeeeevil.*

Barefoot and shirtless, wearing nothing but tight, tattered pants, Nevos leaned against the railing and ate his kabob. His lips glistened with juice, and his eyes burned with new vigor.

"So what's all this about?" I said, waving at the village with my own kabob. "I mean, I know it's secret and all, but you said something about a cause, right? And recruiting me? Well, how can you recruit me if you don't tell me what you're recruiting me for?"

"Good question."

I laughed. "Yeah? So?"

"You could say we're against the Fae Lords."

"But you *are* a Fae."

"True, but I'm not loyal to Queen Calista. It shouldn't hurt to tell you that much. She knows we're here, after all. Her army can't get at us, but she knows."

"Why can't she get at you? Don't tell me … did Angela make the Veil? Is she the one that sealed off Central Park?"

He took a slurp of beer and shook his head. "No. The truth is we don't know who did. But Angela was already working on developing a special place, a secret place. When she learned that the Fae Lords feared Central Park, she moved her operation here. I … came later."

I took a bit of meat off the stick. The hot tangy flavors filled my mouth, and I washed it down with foamy beer. "So you mean to overthrow the Fae Lords?" I said.

"Something like that."

"But they seem so goodly! Why would you want to do that?"

"Different reasons, I suppose. With Angela, it's about religion. Her gods are the enemies of the gods of the Fae."

"And you?"

His face darkened. "I want revenge."

I blinked. "For what?"

His expression softened, and he waved it away. "Never mind. A story for another time."

Before I could follow up with another question, two figures approached. I instantly recognized them as the taron riders, Nevos's two Fae associates. They bowed their heads to Nevos and one said, "My lord."

"'My lord'?" I repeated, but no one replied. *So it's true.* They were his knights.

"You are well met," Nevos said, clasping each of them by the forearm. "I wasn't sure you'd be able to get away from that worm."

"He was a mighty one," agreed the female.

"Have you seen to your mounts?" Nevos asked.

They nodded. "We also found yours near the roost, waiting, and saw to feeding and stabling him, as well."

"Thank you. I'd just been coming to check on him." I cleared my throat, and he smiled and said, "Lyra and Tae, meet Jade. You remember her from earlier."

Lyra looked me up and down. "Well met, Jade."

"Likewise," I said. They didn't offer to shake or bow, so I didn't, either.

"Well, it's been a long day, and I'm sure we could all use our rest," Nevos said. "Let's find Jade accommodations, then return to Angela's."

"Angela's?" I said, as we picked our way through the camp again. Structures blossomed out of the trees around us, not so much like huts as extensions of the trees themselves, only trees didn't have draped windows and doors. They were much finer and more sophisticated dwellings than those on the lower levels of the colony. More magic must have gone into them.

"That's right," Nevos said. "We quarter with Angela. She runs this place, and ... well, you could say that I co-rule it. I'm not second in command, exactly, I'm the other first in command."

"That sounds awkward."

"It is. Which is why I dwell in the Hamptons or elsewhere normally." He chuckled to himself. "I say 'normally', but really I've only been in your world for a few months."

"That's amazing. I thought all the Fae crossed over years ago."

"They did, or most of them. I was late to the party. Here, this should do."

He showed me to a large structure bristling with windows and flooded with sound: plates clacking, people laughing and music playing. Biker-types lounged on terraces along with scantily-clad ladies, while sorcerers smoking hand-rolled cigarettes with glowing smoke leaned on the balcony of others.

"It's one of Angela's nicer hostels," Nevos said. "I'm afraid it's the best I can do on short notice ... unless ... Never mind."

My cheeks burned. I knew all too well what he'd been hinting at. And it *was* tempting, I have to admit.

He left Lyra and Tae outside, escorting me into the interior, which was even louder than outside.

"Don't worry," Nevos said. "Each room has sound dampeners. You won't have to sleep with that in your ears."

"I love magic."

A woman with a red turban and a red dress stood at the counter, admitting guests and seeing to their needs. She checked me in, then showed me to a room on the second floor. It was small but private, and it smelled like resin. All in all, quite nice. And Nevos had been right, it was very quiet inside.

He paused on the threshold. "It's been … interesting," he said, slightly leaning against the doorjamb.

I faced him, standing very close to him. He was still shirtless—didn't he ever get chilly?—and drilling me with those emerald green eyes. Suddenly I realized how hot it was in here.

"Um, yeah," I said lamely.

He started to go, but I reached out and touched his arm. He turned back. He didn't seem as if he were in a hurry to go anywhere. Actually, he looked like he'd rather throw me down on the bed and have his way with me.

It wasn't a bad plan.

Except … and here I could sense threads of my plan coming back together … it couldn't be here. It had to be at Angela's.

"Maybe we could, ah, grab a drink later," I said.

His eyebrows rose slightly. "A drink?" He paused, ruminating on it, and his gaze penetrated me to the core.

I swallowed. "Yeah. Let me settle in, then I could meet you somewhere."

He nodded. "There's a place …" He described it to me and told me where it was, then said, "I'll see you there later."

I watched him go down the noisy wooden corridor, my belly churning both in fear and desire. Davril had claimed that I had some game going, and he'd been right. It had been a stupid game, and so far it had been a disaster. But there was still a chance to right the ship. Er, flip the game board back up? This metaphor is breaking down. But bear with me. There was still a way to fix this mess, and it involved drinks, and possibly more, with a very sexy, very dangerous man.

"Oh, balls," I said, and closed the door.

Chapter 12

The tavern turned out to be quieter than I'd expected. Basically it was just a series of terraces jutting out from one of the huge redwood-like trees that composed much of this area of Shadowpark, and its various levels and directions offered delightful views out over the forest. The terraces were high enough to see over the treetops, at least some of them. It was the highest I'd been yet in Shadowpark.

"Wow," I said. "This is nice."

A fresh breeze blew against me, and I relished it.

"Yes," Nevos said. "Very."

He stood at my side, not quite touching me. Both of us had bottles of beer in our hands. The droplets of moisture from the glass felt cool and nice against my fingers, and I enjoyed the weight of the bottle in my palm.

"Do you drink beer in the Fae Lands?" I asked.

"Ale, certainly. But I mostly drank wine. Although with some whisky and spirits mixed in."

"Whiskey mixed into the wine?" I laughed.

He laughed, too. "Separate. Usually."

I allowed myself to lean into him, just a little. I had a part to play, after all. He was very hot. I mean, temperature-wise. But the other kind, too.

He finally wore a shirt, a loose black silk affair that looked like it might have come from the Fae Lands. The wind pressed against it, etching his hard body and flapping the tails out behind him. Black pants encased his long, muscular legs, but his feet were still bare. His soles must be tough, I thought, eyeing the wooden decking. I'd have gotten splinters in seconds.

Music drifted out to us from deeper in the tavern, but we lingered on the balcony, enjoying the magical night of Shadowpark. Fireflies of a thousand colors—red, green, orange and many more—flickered and flew through the high trees, creating amazing displays. I knew the fireflies weren't your typical varieties but altered with the magic of this place. Shadowpark was dark and deadly, but it was strangely wondrous, too.

"I suppose I've adapted to a lot of your ways," Nevos said. "I mean, the ways of your world."

"The Fae Lords I see on TV are always so stiff and mannered. You don't seem like that at all."

"Ah, it was always my downfall to be different from my brethren. Too impulsive, too rash. Too … other."

"That must have been hard." *What else is hard, Nevvie?*

He shrugged. "I was fine. I'm more interested in you. Jade …. Is that a common name in this world?"

"Not really. Is Nevos common in the Fae Lands?"

One corner of his mouth lifted up. "Not really."

"Well, here's to not really."

I lifted my beer, and we clinked bottle necks. Drank.

"But really," he said. "A magic-using half-shifter thief in New York, the hub of your world. You must have had an eventful life."

"Not so much a half-shifter anymore."

"But more than human."

"Well, I wouldn't go that far," I said. "Call it 'human with benefits'." I laughed at my own joke, but he only smiled. I guessed that reference was a little too out there for even him.

"Someone stole your ability to shift?" he said, wrinkling his brow. When I nodded, he whistled. "That's some serious magic. Especially if it was dragonfire he stole. And I'm guessing it was a he?"

"Yep. You met him earlier."

Nevos took a sip. "Walsh. Yes, I'd wondered. You seemed to know him."

I realized I was giving too much of myself away, and he hadn't revealed anything. "So I understand revenge," I said. "I'm after it, too. What are *you* getting revenge for? Being different?" I said this with a smile to show I was joking, but I kept the smile small just in case that *was* the reason. You never knew, right?

"Not quite," he said.

"Well then?"

He shook his head, and the wind stirred his long black wavy locks. "I don't want to get into all that right now, Jade. Bad memories. I want to think about … more positive things."

His gaze landed on me, and I felt its force and weight fully. I almost staggered under the heaviness of it. His intensity burned into me, heating me up, and my core turned molten. Sheesh, he should bottle that stuff.

I swallowed but forced myself to match his gaze. Softly, so softly a non-supernatural wouldn't have been able to hear, I said, "I'm still here."

That was all it took. His free hand went around my waist and drew me to him. My belly smacked his, sloshing my beer over the side of the railing, but I didn't care. I lifted my face and met his lips with mine. His were eager and hot. He kissed me passionately and firmly, and my blood raced like the fire I would never have again … unless. My free hand played over his hard abs and pecs, at last cupping his face.

His tongue met mine, shoving against it, and I sucked on it greedily.

At last I broke away.

We stared at each other, panting. The desire was a living thing in his eyes.

"Your room," I said. "Now."

I set down the bottle on a nearby table, grabbed Nevos's hand and dragged him down a ramp. Laughing, he drained his drink and set it down, too. In less than a minute we'd left the tavern behind and were making our way back through the camp toward Angela's house. Toward Nevos's bedroom. And the knob.

But at the moment I was thinking of quite a different knob.

The two eyeless witches were on duty beside the treehouse again, but they moved aside as we approached and didn't even bother to greet us. The door swung open. Laughing and kissing, Nevos and I entered. Now he took the lead. Instead of going upstairs, the direction Angela had come from earlier, he took the spiral staircase down, leading down a tight, winding hall, then another. At last he kicked open a thick wooden door framed by vines and led me into his bedroom, his home-away-from-home.

The bed was large, wooden, seemingly grown from the very floorboard, and festooned with flowering vines. The space wasn't large, but it was opulent, and the whole of it smelled with the intoxicating scent of those flowers. I'd never seen their like before.

Nevos shoved me up against the wall and pressed his face to mine.

What am I doing? I thought, feeling Nevos's tongue probe the seam of my lips. He was the enemy!

Davril, forgive me. It's the only way.

Also, I have to confess, I wanted it. Damn it, I really did. Sometimes you just have to go with your instinct.

I tore open his shirt and ran my hands over his taut eight-pack and muscular pecs. Ooo, he was delicious. I could just about eat him up.

He trailed kisses down from my lips to my neck, and I almost whimpered when his lips touched the soft skin there.

Then, breathless, he pulled back.

"Are you sure?" he said.

I reached down and unzipped him, then pulled out his cock, which had become hard. It was huge and thick, and it pulsed in my grip. I wanted it in me. Now.

"I'm sure," I said. "Besides, what else are we going to do till morning?"

Nevos grinned ruefully. "A bad girl. Just my type."

He swept me up in huge arms like I was weightless, pressing me against his chest as though I were a young girl, or maybe a groom carrying his bride over the threshold, then marched to the huge bed and threw me down on it.

He kissed my cheek, then down my throat again, and I hastily shrugged off my shirt. He helped lift it over my head, and I tossed it aside gladly, then reached around and unfastened my bra strap. Sent it sailing on top of the shirt. My nipples stiffened at the contact with the cold air, and goose bumps popped out on my breasts. He kissed them, and I sighed when his tongue made circles around a nipple, then flicked it fast-fast-fast.

"Ahh," I moaned.

I was in a hurry now. I kicked off my shoes and socks, unbuttoned my jeans and tugged them down. He helped, jerking them off in a rush, then, more gently helped me pull my panties down. Sure enough, they were drenched.

His nostrils quivered, scenting the moistness with his supernatural senses, and I blushed. He only grinned wider. He knelt between my splayed legs, his eyes on my crevice. I wished I had shaved my patch before showing up at the rooftop bar earlier today, but that had been the last thing on my mind. At least I'd done my legs. It didn't seem to bother him.

"Are you really going to … ?" I started.

"You know it."

He grabbed my thighs and threw my legs over his broad, sexy shoulders, then kissed my belly. His warm tongue made circles around my navel, then trailed kisses down to my mound. My breaths came faster and faster. *Am I really doing this? I just met this guy!* But I knew enough. He had just saved my life from Walsh, and he had proven himself a fearless, brave hero of the highest order, however rogue. He might be more villain than hero, but he was a worthy bed partner.

I gasped when he lapped my crevice with his tongue, slowly running it up from the lowest part to the highest. Then he started again at the bottom, but this time he pressed his tongue inside me, just a bit. Delicious tingles radiated all throughout me. He lapped me again, and I moaned and squeezed my thighs together, then gripped his wavy black hair in one hand while I squeezed one of my breasts with the other.

"You like that?" he said, looking up from between my legs. Moisture rimmed his lips.

"Uh-huh," I said, breathless. Nodding.

He held up a thick finger, and a smile played at the corner of his lips.

"Know what I'm going to do with this?"

I bit my lower lip and shook my head.

Amusement danced in his eyes as he placed the finger at my opening, then inserted it inside me—but only one knuckle deep. I gasped and squirmed, loving the feel of him inside me, even just a little. He was such a tease. I cried out as he plunged his thick, calloused finger deeper into me, then I grabbed a pillow and shoved it over my mouth. I didn't know if Angela or the other Fae could hear, but it paid to be safe. I moaned into the pillow as he thrust his finger into me all the way, and I gripped it with my vaginal muscles. If his finger was this thick, how big would his dick be? I couldn't wait to find out.

His tongue caressed my clit, and I gasped and clutched the pillow to my chest. His finger pulled out, then plunged in again—hard!—even as his tongue continued to lap my nub, and waves of pleasure coursed through me. I arched my back and moved my hips gently, opening myself to him. One of his hands stroked the side of my face, and I brought his fingers to my lips and kissed them. Then I placed that hand on my breast. Getting the message, he rubbed my nipple with his thumb, and it stiffened even more. The pressure built and built in me, and I knew I couldn't last much longer.

"No!" I said. "Stop."

He kept doing what he was doing for a moment, then paused and looked up.

"Are you sure?"

"I want you inside me," I said.

"I can arrange that."

Slowly, he stood, trailing kisses up my thighs, then my knees and all the way to my feet as he unfolded. When he was fully up, his cock jutted up proudly, and I moaned again when I saw the bead of white fluid gathered on the tip. Impishly, I sat up and brought my mouth to it. Sitting down like I was, I was at the perfect height for what I wanted to do. I didn't kiss the head of his shaft immediately but kissed its sides, running my lips all the way down to its base.

"What are you doing?" he said, but I could hear the pleasure in his voice and knew what he really meant was *What are you doing to me?*

I loved it. Here he was, this big, confident, muscular Fae Lord, and I was driving him wild. I had complete power over him, of his pleasure, and he was willingly giving me that power.

I stroked his balls gently with one hand while the other gripped his muscular thigh, stabilizing myself, then licked the bead of pearly white from the head of his dick. It was salty and delicious. As soon as I stroked his shaft with my tongue again, his cock pulsed and another bead replaced it.

"You like that?" I said.

It was his turn to say, "Uh-huh."

His face had gone rigid, his eyes burning brands. He was *into* this!

Smiling, I opened my mouth wide and took him inside me. I made circles around the head of his shaft with my tongue, then made my lips seal tight to either side of his enormous shaft. I bobbed my head down, taking him deeper inside me, then back up, then back down again. He moaned above, and I felt his huge, cum-filled balls pulse in my hand. His giant cock throbbed in my mouth, and I could taste more of his pre-cum on my tongue.

I took him inside until I couldn't take him anymore, then removed my hand from his balls and wrapped it around the base of his shaft. I squeezed it and pumped up and down even while I continued to bob my head, and he let out a long, low sound. It was such a damn sexy sound I felt myself getting even wetter than I already was, and I wouldn't have thought that was possible.

"No more," he gasped at last. "No more or I'll ..."

I teased him by making one more circle around his shaft with my tongue. His cock throbbed again, and I tasted more pre-cum in my mouth. When his dick throbbed, his abs convulsed, too, and I loved the way his eight-pack rippled. He craned his head and grit his teeth, and cords of muscle stood out on his thick neck. I knew he was struggling hard not to come.

"Not yet," I said, pulling back. I blew on his dick, as if to cool it off, and looked up at him, all quivering muscles and intense eyes. He had been right on the brink.

I leaned back in the bed, spreading my legs, and he dropped to his knees before me. His cock rubbed my opening as he bent over me, and he kissed me on the lips even as the head of his shaft shoved, just an inch, inside. I moaned into his mouth and threw my legs around his waist, just barely managing to hook my ankles together on the other side.

"Is this what you want?" he said, shoving just a little deeper into me.

I nodded and ran a hand up his abs, relishing his tight muscles, and paused in the valley between his mighty pecs. I could feel his heart beating fast and strong beneath my fingers. The gleam of sweat beaded his brow.

"I want you," I said. "Now."

"Will you lay a spell on me if I don't?"

I snorted a laugh, not very lady-like. "I might! Now put that thing inside me right now or so help me—"

He grinned and shoved himself inside me. I bit the inside of my cheek to prevent crying out. He pushed in deeper, stretching me, but even though it hurt a little the pleasure was so intense that hardly mattered. I closed my eyes, delighting in the feel of him. He was huge, bigger than any man I'd ever had before. I could already feel my vaginal muscles quivering around him. He pulled back, then rolled his hips, stroking into me. With every pump, he thrust deeper and deeper. He filled me completely, or what I thought was completely, and then his cock throbbed with a titanic pulse, stretching me even more.

"Yes," I heard myself say. "Yes."

I opened my eyes to see him bending over me. That intense, sexy look was back on his face, and I could see his eyes shift colors as he kissed my breasts and trailed kisses up my neck to behind my ear. I moved my hips, taking him deeper, then pulling back, then deeper again. We matched rhythms, going faster and faster, harder and harder. The bed rocked beneath me, and I had to adjust my balance to keep it quiet.

The pressure built and built in me again, carrying me to maddening heights, and finally I couldn't take it anymore. I bit his chest to stifle my cries as I exploded around his shaft, and my orgasm triggered his own. He groaned and went rigid as his cock throbbed inside me, again and again, shooting hot jets deep into me. His seed filled my core. Still entranced in my own aftershocks, I kissed his sweaty chest and ran my hands through his hair.

Both panting, we collapsed to the bed, and I draped an arm across his chest as we recovered. His seed trickled out of me, and I had to fight a naughty desire to slip a finger down there and taste it. Fae jism!

"Wow," Nevos said, turning his head sideways to peer into my eyes. "That was intense."

I kissed the side of his chest. He had wrapped an arm around me, bringing me in close, and despite the nearness of danger I had never felt so protected.

"That was wild," I said, then confessed, "I've never done anything like this before."

"Me, either."

I studied him. I almost thought I believed him.

He yawned. "Well, I'm exhausted after that. You want to sleep here?"

"Yes, please. I couldn't move if I had to."

He grinned. "That's what all the ladies say afterward."

I laughed and punched his arm. He laughed, too. That made me feel even worse about what I was about to do.

Shortly we settled in and he started to breathe deeply and regularly. When I knew he was asleep, I slipped out of bed. I hadn't lied. My legs were still shaky. He had been really, really good.

Would Davril be as good? Better?

You'll never know if he finds out about this.

I sighed, staring down at the sleeping Nevos. He was so gorgeous, so brave and commanding. It was a shame he was on the other side. Hell, one of their leaders!

I had to do what I had to do.

I pulled my cat burglar outfit back on and crept out of Nevos's bedroom. Now time to find the knob.

Chapter 13

Angela's lair was dark and silent as I slipped like a shadow through its halls. I could feel her magic everywhere. Magic traps had been installed in every nook and cranny. Fortunately Nevos had rendered me immune from them on the way in. But the ones upstairs? I wasn't sure about those.

I went slowly. Cautiously. Everything could be riding on what I was about to do. That is, if I could even do it.

The floorboard squeaked under my foot. I paused, stiffening. I glanced all around. I was almost to the staircase.

No one appeared to drag me away, so I inched forward. I reached the spiral staircase and started upward. My legs were still wobbly, and it was so dark even my shifter senses had difficulty picking out the way. Obviously this was some sort of magical gloom. Angela would have a ring or a bracelet or something that enabled her to see in it just fine. She must "put out the gloom" every night after a certain time, like a curfew for her guests. *No blundering about after 2 a.m., assholes.* Something like that.

Going more cautiously, I inched my way up the stairs. My belly churned, and bile stung the back of my throat. Fear had laid a cold clammy claw around my throat. *Shit, this is a bad idea, Jade. Getting laid I can understand, but getting killed is a no-go. Turn back! Turn back!*

I shoved the cowardly voice in my head down and continued on. I reached the main level, the floor that apparently served as Angela's living area, or at least her guest area. From here the stairs would either take you up or down. I glanced around, peering into every shadow. I expected to see a bunch of feathery heaps where the Razor Wings were camped out, or maybe the eyeless witches, but I saw nothing.

Not daring to breathe a sigh of relief, I continued upward, moving with all the grace and silence my abilities allowed me. *Don't fail me now.* My skin crawled as I neared the third floor, what had to be Angela's level. Her lair. The taste of bile grew even stronger in the back of my mouth, and I swallowed convulsively. When I reached out to grip the guardrail of the stairs, I saw that my fingers were trembling. *Suck it up, girl! You got this!*

I so didn't have this. This was, like, epically bad. My game had taken some weird turns, and now I was compelled to see this thing through. Or else.

Or else *what?* Just what the hell *was* the knob, and what did it do?

Hoping I would find answers, I forced myself to the top of the stairwell. Here at last I was on the top level of the spooky treehouse. The darkness pressed even thicker here, more opaque and more cloying.

The stairwell had come up at the end of a hall, and several doors branched off from it. An especially large doorway loomed at the far end, just visible in the darkness. Probably Angela's suite, I thought, but I wouldn't put it past her to use a fake-out room, either. To go into that room could be to be lured into a trap.

I hunched low and moved away from the stairway. I crept extra slowly now, aware that there could be more magical booby-traps that I wouldn't be immune to. Sure enough, I sensed one right ahead of me: a force field spanning the breadth of the hall, sealing off any part of it past this point.

I concentrated hard, sensing it fully, then extracted one of the new spellgredients from my utility belt. The resin from the drool of a certain poisonous frog. I mixed that with the pulped spores of a magic mushroom, then said a spell under my breath as I cast the combined powder at the force field. It shimmered brightly, startling me, and for a moment I thought it was going to hold. If it did, I was screwed. I didn't know any spells more powerful than that one. Maybe Ruby would have, but not me.

The shield dissolved, and I slumped in relief.

Still on high alert, I edged forward. I passed a doorway and held out my palm to sense what was beyond it. I'd gotten a bead on the emanations of the knob everyone was so excited about, and I was pretty sure I would be able to sense it again. Hopefully it would be somewhere other than with Angela. I didn't want to have to tangle with her if I didn't have to.

Nothing. At least not behind that door.

I moved on. I checked the next room, then the next. Twice more I disabled magical traps. At last I hunched beside the door at the end of the hall. Closing my eyes, I held out my hand, trying to pick up a tingle …

Bingo!

The knob was on the other side of that door.

I opened my eyes and stared at it. I could hear nothing, sense nothing from the room beyond the door other than the knob. Damn it, I was going to have to go in and just pray it wasn't Angela's bedroom.

First I inspected the doorknob of the room. Shockingly it was unlocked. That was either a very good sign, a sign of Angela's overconfidence, or else a very bad sign. Hoping it was the former, I reached out, grabbed the doorknob, which was surprisingly cool under my fingers, and turned it. I held my breath as I cracked the door. Nothing jumped out at me and no alarms blared, so I opened it further, wide enough so that I could see what was on the other side.

It seemed to be a suite of rooms, with a short hallway leading to a larger chamber with more doors coming off of it. I slipped inside and closed the door behind me.

Deep breath.

Turning, I pressed my back against the wall and skulked toward the larger area. I passed a doorway I hadn't noticed earlier. The shadows were very thick. Fortunately nothing grabbed me from its shadowed interior; the doorway was open.

Ahead I began to hear sounds. Not only was visibility muted here, but sound was, too. The sounds seemed to be chanting ... some sort of spell? Interesting. Angela must still be at the "working", as she had called it. A common enough word, really. Something witches and wizards used to describe a complicated spell or series of spells. Why did she have to perform a spell on the knob? And I was only assuming that's what she was doing.

Curious but as tense as I had ever been, so wired I wasn't even blinking, I moved forward. I came within sight of the larger chamber.

Sure enough, Angela stood in the middle of it, right before a stone pedestal with a crimson pillow on it. The knob rested on top. Angela did have style, I had to give her that. Wearing the same red dress as earlier, she gestured and thundered, and the room shook at the power of her exertions.

"Curum thurugris listrum!" she shouted. I could hear the volume of her words now. The magic muting them had been dispelled with proximity. As she spoke, she waved a wand before the knob, and it glowed green. Her skin was flushed and her auburn hair sweaty. She'd obviously been at this for awhile. Judging by the bright glow of the knob, she must be nearly finished with her working.

Shit. That meant there was still a chance to stop her before she completed it. And that meant I would have to do something stupidly heroic.

Why couldn't I have picked an easier line of work?

I unholstered my small crossbow from my hip and centered the aim on Angela's back. I hated to shoot anyone in the back, but Angela was too powerful for anything less than a surprise attack. It was a shot in the back or nothing.

I took a step forward, getting a better aim … held my breath … started to squeeze the trigger …

I stiffened as cold sharp metal bit into the soft flesh of my neck.

A man's voice said in my ear, "I wouldn't do that if I were you."

Nevos.

Gently, I lowered the crossbow and turned to him. His face was tight and hard to read, but I sensed hurt there.

"How stupid did you think I was?" he said.

"It wasn't like that," I said.

"I knew you were a thief. But I thought you had *some* honor."

"No, really, it wasn't …"

Behind me Angela's chants had ended. I heard her sharp footsteps as she strode toward us. Angrily, she spun me around, grabbed the crossbow and smashed it against the wall. It shattered into a thousand pieces.

"You little slut!" she said. "Did you really think you could kill me and take it for yourself?"

"Well, I was hoping."

She backhanded me across the face. Pain flared through me, and I fell backward. Nevos caught me, careful not to stab me with his knife, then set me on my feet again. I wobbled and blinked up at Angela, who was a few inches taller than me. She glared down at me out of that cute freckled face. She looked younger than she had even earlier, younger even than Blackfeather.

As if to think of that name had summoned some recollection, Angela's eyes widened in shock. "You!" she said.

My glamour must be fading. She could see my real face now.

Nevos turned my head and swore.

"A glamour!" he said. Then, sadly, "You look even more lovely now, Jade. If that is your real name."

"Oh, it is," seethed Angela. "Jade McClaren. One of the McClaren sisters. I was wondering how many Jades there were when we were introduced. *She's the one that killed my daughter!*"

I didn't drop my eyes. "I was aiming at you."

She backhanded me again. This time I flew against the wall. I rebounded and punched her in the jaw. She took the blow and kneed me in the stomach. I doubled over, gasping, the taste of vomit shooting into my mouth. I reached for one of the pouches on my belt, but Nevos's strong hands grabbed my arms and stilled them. He pulled me back up against his body, and his hot breaths teased my ear.

"I was hoping you were being honest with me," he said. Genuine regret filled his voice. He *had* liked me, then.

I spat blood at Angela's feet. "Then you shouldn't have hooked up with *her*," I said. "And with her Master."

Angela sneered. "You don't want her, Nevos. She's the partner of your brother."

"*What?*"

"That's right. I've made a great study of her, as much as I can, anyway. I've had my spies ferret out as much information as they could. I was hoping I could discover where she lives and steal her and her sister away, and thereby get my revenge. I didn't manage that much, but I did learn some very interesting things."

"Such as?"

"She was made an honorary Fae Knight and was partnered with your brother. I believe one of her goals, other than stopping us, has been to find Vincent Walsh and steal back the ring containing her fire. After getting her revenge on him, that is."

Nevos's voice was soft. "So you didn't lie about that, at least."

I let out a breath. "You've got me. Now what are you going to do with me?"

* * *

I screamed as fire consumed me. Every cord of my body stood rigid, and I shook with pain. My lungs were sore from screaming. At last the agony retreated, and I gasped and shuddered. My cat burglar outfit was shredded and clung to my sodden body, and my hair fell in wet tangles to either side of my face.

Angela stalked back and forth before me, fury warping her features. In one hand trailed the flaming length of a magical whip. Composed of mystical fire, it inflicted the agony of flame without actually burning me. That would kill me too quickly, and Angela wanted this to last.

"Bitch!" she shouted. "Murderous whore of a she-beast!"

She lashed her whip again, striking me across the chest. I arched my back and screamed. My hands were bound above my head, and I hung from the ceiling of one of the rooms I'd passed on the way to the Chamber of the Knob. It didn't surprise me at all that one of them was a torture chamber.

"You took my only daughter from me, and now you will know my pain," Angela went on.

Through gritted teeth, I said, "I'm sorry about Blackfeather. She shouldn't have gotten in the way. She was worth ten of you."

She screamed and lashed me again. The fire coursed along my side. I tried not to cry out, but the pain was too great. Shuddering, I glared at her, wishing Nevos were here. He had argued against torturing me. Of course that probably meant he was simply in favor of executing me, but that sounded better than being Angela's plaything.

Only, as it turned out, it wasn't merely my physical pain she was after.

"Tell me, you whore," she said.

"Tell you what, cunt?"

Strike! When the agony retreated, she said, "Your sister. Ruby. Tell me where to find her and I'll stop."

I sucked in a breath, let it out. "So that's your plan, is it? You want to torture Ruby to death in front of me? Think that will make things even? Well, it won't. I'm sorry. I've lost loved ones before, and I know how therapeutic the idea of revenge is. But loss is just something you have to deal with."

"So you would turn down Vincent Walsh if I offered him to you? I think not."

She had a point. "Ruby is innocent."

"So was Blackfeather."

"She helped you in both Voris Cemetery and the raid on the Palace. She probably killed plenty of good people to further your mad quest."

Strike! Pain consumed me, like waves pounding a rocky beach, then gradually ebbed. But I knew another wave would come soon enough.

"Ruby has assisted you on plenty of your criminal jaunts," Angela said. "She's no innocent. Now tell me where she is!" She coiled her whip arm, daring me to hold out on her. "Tell me now!"

With all the courage I still possessed, I met her livid gaze. "Go. To. Hell."

She screamed. The whip came down. White-hot agony wrapped around me, smashing me into a million splinters, then glued me back together again only for me to go through it all again. Angela lashed me and lashed me until all I knew was pain.

Finally, exhausted, she lowered the weapon, flipped a lock of sweaty auburn hair out of her face and stared at me. "You might not break today, Jade McClaren. But you'll break eventually. They all do. And then things will get very interesting."

Her lips twisted in a cruel half smile. I would have given some retort, but I was too drained to speak. I could barely draw breath. I was a shuddering, bloody, sweaty mess. The whip hadn't burned me, but it had certainly cut my flesh.

"I'll be back," Angela said.

She gathered her whip into a coil and stalked from the room, slamming the door behind her. I stared at it for a long time, expecting her to burst back in, laughing manically, but she didn't, and at last I slumped in guarded relief. Not that I could do much else than slump.

This was some fine plan you concocted, I told myself. If this was game, I'd lost, that was for sure.

Chapter 14

I only had one ace up my sleeve, and I had to use it wisely.

You see, I was pretty sneaky. When I'd punched Angela earlier, I hadn't used my full shifter strength. I'd hit her with only human-level power. I knew I couldn't overcome both her and Nevos, so I'd tricked her, or tried to. And it had worked. She'd believed that *that's* how strong I was, that I'd had my shifter strength drained away along with my fire.

Luckily the residual strength and speed of a shifter had stuck. It was my only way out now.

When Angela had tied me up, she'd assumed I couldn't draw on any other power to get myself out the bonds. My wrists had been tied together with a magically reinforced cord, and that cord had tied to another magically reinforced cord that hung from the ceiling. The room was small and dark and wooden, with gleaming surgical instruments on trays along the walls. Instruments of torture. I had to get out of here before Angela got around to using those on me. Thanks, but no.

I really was wiped out, though. Torture sounds fun, but it actually sucks.

I waited, panting and bleeding and generally miserable, for a long time before I could summon the energy to do a pull up. Then, slowly and agonizingly, I hauled my body upward. My arms quivered and I cursed like a sailor in my head. I couldn't do it out loud because I didn't have the breath or the strength to curse. It's a pretty sad day when Jade McClaren doesn't have the strength to swear out loud.

Most of the silent curses were directed at myself.

I had been *really* stupid.

Finally I brought my mouth to the rope binding my wrists and wrapped my teeth around them. I bit down. A magical blast filled me, electrocuting me with pain. I cried out and shuddered. A bit of urine trickled down my leg and landed on the floor. Crying, swearing mentally, shuddering and pissing myself, I bit down harder on the rope. More pain filled me. It was heavily warded, and the only thing I had to soak up those wards was my own flesh. Luckily my shifter strength allowed me to chew through the rope, bit by bit. The pain never diminished, but I was used to it after all the whip action earlier. Thanks, Angie.

After what seemed like twenty years but was probably just a few minutes, the rope parted.

I fell in a wet heap to the floor, smack in the middle of my own piss and blood. I moaned, tried to get up, and collapsed. I lay there for a long time, wishing I were dead, then managed to sit up.

I took stock. I couldn't go through the door. That portal would be heavily warded, like super dooper fortified. Screw that.

My gaze landed on the wall opposite the door. I was pretty sure that on the other side of that door was the outdoors. If I could get through that wall, I might have a chance. I didn't have my spellgredients, and I knew the wall would be enspelled, too. Luckily I knew a spell that might help using only my blood and urine. Again, thanks, Angie.

Gathering a small palmful of each fluid, I dragged myself over to the wall. I smeared a circle of blood on the wall, then overlaid it with a circle of pee. *The Great Pee Escape*, I could hear Ruby calling this later. Well, that was fine. If I could get out of this, she could call it whatever she liked.

As I smeared the second circle, I said a chant under my breath. The circle began to glow. I said another series of words, laid my palm in the middle of the circle, and closed my eyes, funneling my reserves of strength and concentration into that section of the wall. A bright light flashed, and the wall within the stinky circle vanished. I lurched forward, off balance.

Cool night air washed in, bathing my face. I blinked, relishing it. My blood quickened, enlivened at the idea of escape. I could get out of here. I *would* get out of here.

The missing portion of the wall would rematerialize in a few seconds. I barely had the strength to slither through that hole, but I sucked it up and slid out, flopping to the walkway on the other side just as the circle popped back into being. Hopefully the interruption in magical energies had been so brief that Angela wouldn't have been alerted. But I couldn't count on it.

Problem was I couldn't walk, or even stand.

And how the hell was I going to get out of here?

"Looks like you have a problem."

Chills raced up and down my spine. The voice, like before, belonged to Nevos. Dreading what I would see, I glanced up.

Nevos Stormguard, once heir to a kingdom, mighty Fae Lord and arch-traitor, leaned against the railing of the walkway smoking a hand-rolled cigarette. The tip glowed briefly, and smoke trailed up.

"How long have you been there?" I managed. Speech proved difficult but possible.

"Long enough." A small smile cut through his five o'clock shadow. "Angela and I agreed that you might try to escape, so I decided to post myself here."

Despair washed over me. All that effort, for nothing. They had been one step ahead of me the whole time. I slumped even lower than before. Tears burned behind my eyes, but I refused to let them out.

A faint crackling sound—Nevos's cigarette. He watched me calmly, silently. Around us the camp had settled in for the night. A few toughs and mages strolled the ramps and walkways of the outlaw village, and some rock music blasted from a treehouse two levels down that must be a whorehouse, still going this late in the evening (however late that was—I wasn't quite sure), but muted by walls and distance.

Gasping, I lurched up and put my back to the wall I'd just crawled out of. I stared at his cigarette.

"Got another?" I said.

"Didn't know you smoked."

"Used to. Quit. Now it doesn't matter."

"That's rather defeatist," he said. Still, he pulled out some papers and some tobacco and rolled one for me. He put it to my lips, then lit it with a snap of his fingers.

I inhaled gratefully. It was the first smoke I'd had since Ruby made me quit more than a year ago. The nicotine hit my bloodstream and I grinned tiredly despite everything.

"Thanks," I said.

"Sure."

I blew a plume of smoke at him, imagining it was my old dragonfire. As if realizing the jest, he raised a palm as if to deflect it with his magic. We both smiled, but they were small smiles.

A long moment passed. I smoked. Music drifted. Somewhere an owl hooted.

"Tell me," Nevos said. "Is it true about you and … Davril?"

"It's true that he's my partner."

"You mean, as a Fae Knight. Not … anything else?"

I watched him. "No. Not anything else."

He seemed to think about that. "Is that because you don't want him? No, I can see it in your face. You do want him. Does he … yes, he does, doesn't he? Then why?"

I didn't answer. He studied me carefully. I got the feeling this was important somehow, though I didn't understand how. Maybe he didn't want Davril's leavings. Who knows. Guys are weird. At the moment, I couldn't give two fucks. My plan was to finish my smoke, then throw myself over the rail. I wouldn't allow myself to be tortured into giving up Ruby's location. I didn't think Angela could make that happen with pain, but she was very powerful magically. I'm sure if she tried hard enough she could use some spell or artifact to loosen my tongue, however unwilling I was.

"You look like someone who could use a friend," Nevos said.

"Go to hell."

"No, I'm serious." He leaned forward, just slightly. "Did you sleep with me just because you wanted inside Angela's treehouse?"

I eyed the glowing end of my cigarette. I said nothing.

"There was something there, wasn't there?" he said. "Between us?"

I sucked in a long drag, then blew the smoke at the stars. "Maybe," I admitted.

"I knew it!" He smiled. Then he looked at me, and his enthusiasm faded.

"Sorry," I said. "I know I'm not at my peak right now. Just need to powder my nose and I'll be fine. Maybe use the dryer on my hair. No big deal. Don't let the blood and stench of urine put you off."

"I was trying to be gentlemanly and not mention it."

He said it lightly, humorously. Surprising myself, I laughed a little.

"You're all right sometimes," I said.

"Only sometimes?" His eyebrows shot up, as if I'd wounded him.

"Well, you *are* evil."

"*Evil* is a tad harsh."

"You do serve the Shadow. Unless I've been greatly misinformed." For a moment doubt rose up in me. Was it possible that I'd been lied to the whole time, that I was really on the wrong side of this conflict? Maybe Nevos had been in the right all along.

"No," he said. "I do. I serve the Shadow."

Or maybe not.

"Why?" I said. "The Shadow overran the kingdoms of the Fae. Killed countless of your kind. Subjected many others and drove the rest out of your world entirely. Now you're here, helping the Shadow bring ruin to the few that remain? I'd call that evil. And I *don't* feel bad about using you." Although I did.

He drew in the last drag of his cigarette, then stubbed the butt out. Standing, he moved toward me.

He held out a hand to me.

"Time to take me back in, is it?" I said. Well, this was it. I'd put the cigarette out on his hand and jump over the railing while he was distracted. Goodbye, cruel world. At least I'd gotten laid before I left it. And it had been pretty good, too.

"Maybe not." His voice was low and strange.

So strange that I switched my gaze from his hand, which I'd been about to strike, to his eyes. They were dark. Conflicted. But a resolution was growing there.

Feeling as if I were in a dream, I offered him the hand not holding the cigarette and allowed him to help me to my feet. I was still weak and unsteady, and he had to put his hands to my sides and make sure I didn't fall over. His hands were strong and firm.

I blew a cloud of smoke in his face.

"What are you talking about?" I said.

"I may serve the Shadow, Jade, but you don't know everything. You don't know what happened between me and Davril. You don't know what's going on here with Angela and I."

"You two have something going?"

He started to remove his hands. I listed to the side, and he caught me. I still had one drag left. One last chance to use my cigarette to help me get away … for the brief moment I needed.

"That's not what I mean," Nevos said. "We both serve Lord Vorkoth, but for different reasons. And we both want to be the one that brings him victory."

I blinked tiredly. "So you and Angela … are enemies?"

"She needed my help in finding the knob. I needed hers in using it. Now that time has come." He patted his hip pocket, and to my shock I saw a bulge there.

"Is that … is that *it?*" I said. I couldn't have been more surprised if Hugh Grant had shown up wearing a tube top.

"Yes. I helped myself to it on the way out."

"What … does that mean?" I tried to analyze his face, but it was swimming in and out of focus. Was I about to pass out? Great. Dredging up my last brain cells, I said, "Are you …. busting out of here?"

"Yes. And I was weighing whether or not to take you with me." He cupped my cheek with his palm. "You know, I like this face better."

His lips were very close. I pulled back. He let me.

"Do you want to go with me?" he said.

"Where … to? What does the knob do?"

"Opens a door," he said, smiling. "What else? Now, I need an answer, Jade. It will be dangerous, and there could be—"

"Yes! For the love of God, yes! Get me the fuck out of here! Just promise me that there will be a shower at the other end of this ride."

"Well, I didn't want to be the first one to say it."

He kissed me. His lips were full and hot, and I kissed back. My brain reeled, with dizziness, exhaustion, pain and just sheer surprise, but his kiss oriented me somehow. Pulling away from him, I took the last hit off the cigarette and stubbed it out.

"You'll need this," he said and handed me something.

Dully I realized it was my utility belt. Trying not to sob in relief, I strapped it around my waist, reassured at its familiar weight. Now at last I could defend myself.

"There!" someone shouted. "There they are! Get them!"

"Shit," I said.

Before I could prepare myself, footsteps rushed toward us.

Chapter 15

"Was this part of the plan?" I said.

He grabbed my hand and hauled me along the walkway. I stumbled, righted myself and ran just behind him. Adrenaline flooded my system, restoring some of my sorely needed clarity. And coordination. At the moment, that was perhaps even more important.

I bounced off a guardrail as I ran and tried to move in a straight line. Shouts were coming from all over.

"There!" someone said. "I see them!"

"I take it this wasn't part of your plan," I panted.

"Not entirely."

We ran over a bridge to a walkway on the far side. Half a dozen biker-types gathered there, brandishing guns and knives and chains.

"Stop right there!" the leader said. "We're not supposed to let you through."

Nevos placed his hand to his hip, and suddenly I saw he was wearing a sword there, slim and gorgeously wrought. Had it just materialized? Was that a Stormguard thing? He pulled out the sword and it glimmered with strange lights.

"Come and get me."

The biker leader sneered. "Drill him, boys."

The three members of his gang that carried pistols raised them. I braced myself. After all I'd gone through to die by gunfire almost seemed laughable. I wished I still had my crossbow. Even my shifter strength and speed had deserted me, at least for the moment.

Nevos raised his free hand, the one not holding the sword. Light flashed out. The bikers staggered back, gasping and dropping their weapons. I'd seen Davril perform the same feat once in Walsh's adopted penthouse. I knew he could only do it once until the power regenerated, which took time.

Looking wearied, Nevos said, "Come."

He resumed running across the bridge, and I followed. When I reached the fallen bikers, who were moaning and stirring feebly, I reached down and grabbed the knife off one and shoved it through my belt. I grabbed the pistol off another.

"Thanks for the donation," I said.

Bird shrieks made my head snap up.

"Damn," said Nevos.

Three Razor Wings in bird form raced at us. In the open area between trees where the bridge was, they could be quite effective. I started to raise my gun, but there was no time to aim, and they could heal fast anyway.

Nevos and I ran. We reached the end of the bridge and took a turn. He fled up a ramp. Goons spilled out from doorways of huts. Some shouted or lunged at us. I kicked one over the side of the rail. Nevos chopped one down with his sword.

A magical ball of energy smashed into the wooden decking near my feet. I glanced around to see a mage coiling his wand for another strike. Already fiery energy gathered at the wand's tip.

I shot him through the head. He crumpled to the floor, dead.

"Hurry!" Nevos said. "We're almost there."

"Almost where?"

He didn't answer. Bird shrieks reached my ears again as we fled, and glancing over my shoulder I saw the Razor Wings still on our trail. They couldn't come in close because of the tree limbs, though. Good. But how were we going to get out of this? Usually when you kick a beehive you should have plans to be far away by the time the bees start to swarm. You don't kick a beehive *in the middle of the beehive*. Whatever Nevos's plan was, it had obviously gone horribly wrong somehow.

Two shapes materialized ahead: Lyra and Tae, Nevos's knights.

"This way!" said Lyra. She fired what looked like an old-fashioned blunderbuss into the face of an oncoming warrior in black leather. Instead of gun smoke, magical green light flashed out. The warrior dissolved from the top down, becoming a puddle of goo. Steam rose from the remains.

"Damn," I said.

"The mounts are ready?" Nevos said.

"They're champing at the bit, my lord," said Tae.

"Good!" Nevos threw a tiny knife at a mage taking aim at us with his wand on a nearby platform.

I shot at a witch as we ran, taking a turn. Lyra and Tae led up a ramp and onto a platform that served as a roost: all sorts of winged creatures were tied up here, from giant crows and bats to the Fae's tarons. They cawed eagerly at seeing us. Lyra and Tae jumped astride theirs, and Nevos did his, too, then patted the seat behind him.

"With us, Jade!"

As if I had a choice. Shit, I was still wobbly. I crawled behind him and held on as he gave the dinosaur-like flying creature his heels. It took off with a furious flapping of scaly, leathery wings. We shot into the skies, Lyra and Tae just behind us.

"Blast!" said Lyra. "They're right on our heels!"

I craned my head. Sure enough, a dozen Razor Wings flew in a wedge formation aimed at us. Three of them were occupied by riders, all women—more Razor Wings, but unshifted so they could use their magic better.

One of the witches hurled a blue fireball at us. Nevos jerked the reins, pulling his taron to the side. The fireball whizzed past.

Lyra shot the witch's mount with her blunderbuss. The great bird dissolved as if hit by acid and fell from the sky. The witch that had shot at us leapt off its back and shifted, becoming what her mount had been. At least she couldn't shoot at us in this form. But her beak and talons were deadly sharp, I knew all too well.

The Razor Wings were fast, magically so.

"We can't outrun them," I said.

Lyra shot another, and another. Tae threw bursts of deadly energy at them. I fired my gun until it was empty, then tossed it to the treetops below. The Razor Wings drew on, closer every second.

"Damn," said Nevos. "We're going to have to set down. Lose them in the trees."

He angled his taron downward, and Lyra and Tae followed suit. My stomach lurched and I pressed my thighs tighter against the dino's flanks. It was hot and leathery where I could touch it, but the saddle was well-made and comfortable enough. To steady myself, I wrapped my arms around Nevos's middle. That was the only reason, I swear.

His taron issued a loud caw as we swept beneath a thick limb and through the twisted maze of wood that comprised the forest canopy. Lyra swore behind us, and I heard wood breaking. The spaces between limbs were very narrow. We couldn't survive here long.

The Razor Wings shrieked in rage above us but didn't follow us in, at least not for the moment. We didn't have long before they sucked it up and pursued, though.

Nevos brought his taron to the ground and set it down. Trailing leaves, Lyra came down behind us, then Tae.

"Gods curse it," Lyra said. "This isn't how it was supposed to go."

We all climbed off the mounts and craned our heads upward. I could just barely see the dark shapes of the Razor Wings flashing above.

"We don't have long," I said.

Nevos grimaced. "We'll leave the tarons here and continue on afoot. But first thing's first." He held out his palm and Lyra's blunderbuss flew through the air and landed in it. She gasped.

Nevos lifted it toward her face, then switched it to Tae. Then again to Lyra. They jumped back and coiled themselves for battle.

"What the hell?" said Tae.

"Which one of you is the traitor?"

"You've gone mad," Lyra said. "We're your most loyal supporters!"

"*One* of you is," Nevos agreed.

"You can't really mean to question us," Tae said.

"Nevos is right," I said. "My escape didn't alert Angela or she would've been after me immediately. Something else—some*one* else—must have tipped her off."

Overhead the Razor Wings shrieked.

"There's no time to do this the proper way," Nevos said. He switched the gun back to point at Tae. "Sorry, my friend."

"No, wait—"

Nevos fired. Blue light flashed and Tae's head exploded, then he began to dissolve. But as he did his body changed. I saw a huge belly encased in black leather with skuzzy boots on the end of his legs.

"A biker!" I said, standing over the puddle of dissolved flesh. As before, steam rose from it.

"One of Angela's," Lyra said. "She must have switched him out with the real Tae." Her face was pale and she was hugging herself. To Nevos, she said, her voice small, "How did you know it was him?"

Nevos handed her back the firearm. "I didn't. It was fifty-fifty."

Anger flashed across her face, but she shoved the weapon away. "Do you think the real Tae is still alive?"

"Maybe," Nevos said.

"He could be in one of the other torture rooms," I said. "Maybe later—"

I fell silent as the shadows of Razor Wings fell over us, even closer now.

"We'll talk about it when we're safe," Nevos said. "Come!"

He took off jogging through the forest. Lyra and I glanced at each other, then followed.

"Poor Tae!" she said, clearly choking down her emotion. "I hope he's still alive. He better be. He—"

A blast of purple lightning arced through the trees and exploded a trunk right before us. I screamed and threw my hands before my eyes. Pieces of woody shrapnel hit me and sliced my hands and shoulders.

"Fuck!"

Lyra picked herself up off the ground. Dark figures rushed toward us through the trees. Damn! The Razor Wings had shifted and were pursuing us on foot. I hated being chased by shifters. If one shape didn't get you, another would. Especially when one was a witch and one a deadly flying creature.

"What are you waiting for?" Nevos said. He'd been just ahead of us and hadn't been hit by the exploding pieces of tree.

I glared at him, aware that pieces of wood were all over me. "Just taking the air," I said.

"Well, come on!"

Another tongue of lightning flashed. A tree exploded beside us, but we were prepared this time. We hunkered low, shielding our heads. Then, when the chaos died down, we resumed running through the woods. Lyra turned to blast one of the witches. The witch dissolved into goo and the other witches ran around her.

Lyra tried to fire her blunderbuss again, but the pistol jammed. She slowed, just for a moment, to examine it, but that was all it took. Another bolt of purple lightning flared out. This one didn't strike a tree but Lyra instead. She screamed, arching her back, and purple electricity coursed up and down her body. I'd turned to throw my knife and saw her eyes bulge and her muscles spasm. Then she crumpled to the ground, smoking and dead.

I started to go to her, but another purple bolt speared out, hitting the ground nearby. I turned and ran. Nevos had stopped to help, and pain showed on his face.

"I'm so sorry," I said, reaching him.

He looked on the verge of going back for her. I knew that would be suicide. I grabbed his hand and pulled him forward. Reluctantly, he went. My heart twisted for him. He'd lost both his loyal followers in a span of seconds.

We ran and ran, the witches right behind us. My heart pounded like a rabid wolf, and sweat dripped down from my hair to sting my eyes. Branches whipped at me. One scratched my cheek, another my arm.

"I see something," Nevos said.

He pointed. I strained my eyes to peer through the scrolling limbs of trees, then made out a high stone wall, dark and somehow grim-looking. Towers jutted up from it at odd points.

"A castle!" I said.

"What would a castle be doing out here?"

He didn't answer. A tree exploded to my left, and I cursed as shrapnel sliced at my arms and legs.

Suddenly, dark shapes materialized in the trees overhead. Eyes flashed, and so did sharp teeth. A weighted net spun through the air, falling right over both me and Nevos. Flailing, we collapsed to the ground, trapped.

The figures disappeared above. Moments later I heard screams and explosions from the direction of the Razor Wings. The same figures that had come after us were making short work of our attackers. Shortly the screams and shouts moved off. The Razor Wings were retreating!

"What the hell?" I said.

I turned to find Nevos's face pressed up against mine. Our bodies were all tangled up against each other. Every time he breathed, I could feel it. Every time I breathed, he could feel it. Our lips were very close to each other.

"Who are they?" I said, my voice low. That wasn't by design, either. I'd suddenly developed a hitch in my throat.

"I don't know," he said, then fingered the net. He seemed to be analyzing its construction. "I think I know this work, though." He turned back to me. A lusty vigor lit his eyes. "You seem to have regained your strength."

"Terror will do that."

He grabbed the links of the net with both hands. Using all his strength, he pulled them apart. Magical energy flared, washing over him, some sort of defense. He grunted but continued pulling.

I added my strength, ripping at the same links he was. Together, we pried the netting apart. At last it tore. Gasping, we stood. My limbs shook with exertion and my eyes still burned with sweat.

"Let's go before they come back," I said.

"Good—"

Before he could even complete the sentence, a ring of dark green figures emerged from the undergrowth. Jagged spears thrust at us, preventing us from leaving. Wicked wands made of bone shards gleamed with exotic magic. I stared in shock at the faces all around us.

"Goblins!" I said.

Chapter 16

"Let me handle this," Nevos said.

"That's right, you've dealt with goblins before."

"Extensively." To the savage green faces all around us, he said, "Who is your leader?"

A tall figure stepped forward. I recognized her instantly.

"Hela!"

Ignoring me, she cocked her right arm, then launched it at Nevos's face. She struck him across the jaw. He absorbed the blow, then shook his head and spat.

"Maybe you don't recognize me," he said. "I'm the Left Claw of the Master. A high servant of the Shadow. A general of goblin hordes, deep in the councils of the Great One."

"Oh, we recognize you," growled Hela. She didn't spare me a glance. To her band, she said, "Take them away!"

They laid their clawed hands on us and shoved us through the forest, in the direction of the castle we'd seen. Great, I thought. Out of the frying pan and into the fire. But what the hell was going on? Nevos was a leader of goblins, a friend to all allies of the Shadow. Or at least I'd thought so. And judging by the frown on his face, he had, too.

My gaze landed on objects mounted atop the castle walls: severed human heads on spikes, dozens of them. Flies buzzed about them.

Bile shot to the back of my mouth. I threw a glare at Hela, but she kept her eyes forward.

The goblins along the wall hooted at seeing the raiding party, if that's what it was, return. The great black gates swung open, and the goblins of Hela's party ushered us through the portal and into a wide muddy courtyard. Goblins went about their business all around. Most were dressed like Hela's group—as medieval soldiers. But the armor seemed mismatched and hodgepodge. Almost more like pirates than soldiers.

Some goblins rode giant green lizards, and they came and went from a large building that was obviously a stable for the creatures. Hela's raiding party hadn't ridden the lizards, but others did.

Hela brought us toward a long low building with iron grates along the windows and brutish guards at every entrance. It didn't take much imagination to see that this was some sort of prison or jailhouse. Hela jerked her head at the building, and the four goblins surrounding Nevos shoved him toward it.

"What's the meaning of this?" he demanded. "You should be bowing to me!"

"We bow to no one," Hela said. "Go on."

The four goblins resumed pushing him toward the jailhouse. Nevos's jaw bulged out, but he didn't try to fight them. There were too many. His eyes found mine. I was surprised to realize that I was actually worried for him. I nodded at him in encouragement. A small smile tugged at his lips, then the guards hauled him away.

I turned to Hela. "Don't I get a cell, too?"

"Do you need one? And yes, I recognize you, even without the glamour. Same clothes, same build, same hair. Same treachery."

I blinked. "So I'm ... not under arrest, or whatever?"

She jerked her head again at the members of her band, and for a moment I thought they were about to seize me and drag me to the jailhouse, too, but instead they saluted her with a thump of their fists on their chests, then broke up, each going their separate ways. She'd simply disbanded them. Now it was just her and me alone in the busy courtyard. Nevos was already out of sight in the jailhouse.

Hela fingered one of the tusks jutting from her mouth. "It was you, wasn't it?" she said. "You struck me on the back of the head and took my sack." Her gaze darted to the sack in question dangling from my hip. It had been attached to the utility belt.

My cheeks burned. I couldn't remember ever being caught so badly.

"Oh, er, this?" I said, patting the sack. "I, ah, just found it ... lying around."

She held out her hand, palm up. I sighed, then unhooked the sack and placed it on her palm. She tied it back at her own waist. Damn. A bottomless sack could've really come in handy.

"Why did you do it?" she said.

"Why did *I* do it?" I echoed. I gestured around me, indicating the walls and buildings. "Why did *you* do it? Who are you? What is all this?" I put some anger into my tone. "You have no right to be interrogating *me*."

She took a step toward me, dwarfing me with her large frame, reminding me that, here, she had all the power.

"I can interrogate you all I want," she said. "And I have some harsh methods by which to do so."

I swallowed. "Oh. Right. I meant that metaphorically." I wiped some imaginary dust off her armor. "You look really cool, by the way. Have any more of those breastplates? And I like what you've done with your, er, scales. They're very … shiny."

Her eyes narrowed. "I'll ask again, why did you attack me and steal the item?"

I sighed. "I wanted to meet a Fae Lord. I wanted to get in good with him. With *them*."

She snorted. "It appears you succeeded. But obviously something went wrong."

"Yeah. We sought out some allies that turned out not to be so friendly." I figured it was better to tell her these things than for her to wring the information out of me. I'd had enough torture for the night. "So what now? You going to kill me?"

She jutted her chin toward the gate, which was still open. "You can go. I don't care why you did what you did. You saved my life aboard the zeppelin. I owe you. But after this, we're even."

I started to take a step toward the gates, then stopped myself. I glanced toward the jailhouse. Nevos was in there somewhere, and he needed me. More than that, I needed him. And not for *that* reason. You have a dirty mind. No, he knew all about the knob and what Angela wanted it for. I needed to know that if I wanted to stop her.

I shuffled my feet and made myself look scared, which wasn't a huge leap. "There are monsters out there," I said.

"Well, duh."

"And I'm alone and virtually unarmed. If you send me out there by myself, it's basically a death sentence. I thought you owed me one."

"Don't tell me what I owe you, Jade."

"Oh. Right. So I guess sending me off to die totally fulfills your warrior code of honor or whatever, huh?"

She stared at me. A flock of bats flew overhead, eclipsing the moon, then flew on. I waited, impatient but trying to hide it.

"Fine," she said at last. "You can stay. At least for a time. I'll take you to the keep and give you a room. But I've got to hurry. My masters will be very interested in learning who I picked up in the forest."

"So your kind really served him in the Fae Lands?" I said as she led the way to the great stone keep dripping in moss and covered in lichen. Ornamental spikes jutted from it, and the whole thing gave off a sinister aura.

"Many of us, yes," she said.

"But *your* people don't."

"No."

She wasn't being very forthcoming. I'd have to try a different tack. "Maybe we could have drinks when you get off shift. You can tell me about it."

She didn't say anything for a minute, then shrugged. "Maybe."

That would have to do.

A large group of goblins drew my attention. They were shouting and hooting at something, but I couldn't tell what. Then I realized they were arranged in a circle and that there was something in the circle. Coming closer, I saw a deep pit with smooth walls and floor. Doors had been carved into the walls. Two huge monsters I wasn't familiar with, both sporting horns and tails, circled each other in the pit, occasionally launching themselves at each other. Blood flew and the goblins laughed or cursed, some exchanging money.

"A gladiator pit," I said.

"My people have always had such sport," Hela said, drawing me away and aiming me back toward the keep.

I shook my head. "It's barbaric."

"We're goblins. 'Barbaric' is a good thing to us. Your soft, civilized ways disgust us."

She brought me to the keep and showed me to a room on the second floor. The goblins quartering there seemed very interested in me, but Hela swore at them and told them to leave me alone.

"As soon as I can spare some troops, I'll have them escort you to the edge of Shadowpark," Hela said. "That's the best I can do."

"That's fine," I said. Of course I had no intention of leaving the castle until I had what I needed—a way to stop Angela.

The room was small and bare, but as soon as Hela was gone I gleefully threw myself on the bed. I was totally wiped out, and my eyes closed almost immediately. When I awoke I felt refreshed and my belly rumbled.

I asked some of the locals where I could get sustenance, but they just grunted at me. Luckily Hela was just getting off her shift, and she found me and brought me to a group of goblins roasting venison over a fire near one of the other keeps; there were several. She thrust a flagon of ale into my hand, and I slurped it while I ate. The meat was juicy and crunchy, and the ale washed it down just right.

"I love waking up to booze," I said.

Hela said nothing. Overhead clouds slithered through the nighttime sky. It was always night in Shadowpark, but it made me wonder just how long I'd been in this crazy place. Davril, Ruby and my other friends were surely worried about me. I had to get out of here, fast. But first things first.

I pulled Hela away from the others and pointed to the jailhouse. "Is Nevos still alive?"

She bit into a hunk of bloody venison. "For now." She grinned around her bite. Blood trickled over her green chin. "My superiors were very happy with me for finding him."

"I still don't get it. Why does your group hate him?"

"Because he's a high servant of the Shadow."

"But don't you serve the Shadow, too?"

"Not us."

I waited for her to go on, but she didn't. I downed some more ale and burped loudly. When in Rome, right? I didn't have any toothpaste or anything else, but I had beer and food. Sadly I knew I could really use a shower and a change of clothes. If nothing else, my new companions would be the last to care about such things.

Even goblins had to shower, though, right?

Instead of grilling Hela about this, I said, "Come on, tell! I mean, you haven't killed me, and you're going to help me get clear of the park, so you're friendly to me, right? So if we're friends, you should tell me the truth."

She watched me carefully, blood still trickling down from the corners of her mouth. She watched me so long I began to feel a chill.

"Well?" I said, hearing the notable loss of enthusiasm in my voice.

"Jade," she said quietly. "You hit me over the head and stole the item."

"Me? Would I do that?"

She tapped the bottomless bag, and I almost slapped my forehead. There was really no way to pretend that I was innocent.

"You showed up here with the client, Jade. Don't take me for a fool. I know the only reason he would have seen you is if you had the knob." A hint of humor touched her eyes. "It's why I wanted to steal it in the first place."

I almost spat out my bite of venison. "You were trying to kill Nevos!"

"When I realized it was him, yes. Until then I was simply going about my duties."

"What duties? I don't understand any of this. Why is there a castle full of goblins in the middle of Central Park, and why were you trying to murder someone who is a leader of your people?"

She let out a long sigh. "I'll tell you the truth if you tell *me* the truth."

I laughed. "My story wasn't very convincing, was it?"

"No."

I fidgeted. How much should I really tell her? Then again, if I told her another lie she would either stop considering me a friend or simply not tell me the truth.

"So you can forgive me hitting you over the head and taking the knob?" I said.

She shrugged again. "I'm a goblin, Jade. We hit each other to say hello."

"Good point. Okay, fine, I'll tell you, but I don't want you to tell this to your superiors or anyone else. This is just between you and me."

She considered that, then nodded. "Very well."

We found a quiet place under a tree and sat down, both of us having refilled our mugs. I sipped often as I told her an abbreviated version of my tale. I finished my drink and my story around the same time. It was an old trick of mine.

"Well?" I said. "Do you see now why it's so important that I speak to Nevos?"

She tilted her head. "You want to stop Mistress Angela. Yes, I understand. But *you* don't understand. Nevos is our enemy, and he must die. Violently."

"But why? What is this all about?" I gestured at the walls and keeps. "Who are you people? Er, goblins?"

"We came from the Fae Lands."

"Duh."

She took a long sip, then leaned back against the tree. Somewhere goblins shouted and a monster in their arena howled. "Most goblins in the Fae Lands worship the Shadow and serve him," Hela said. "But our clan never did. We resisted when His religion began to sweep through our people long years ago. We hid ourselves away and did not traffic with the others of our kind."

"I had no idea."

"When Nevos betrayed the Fae and helped launch the war, we tried to help the Fae."

"Damn!"

"We quickly saw the war was futile, though. But we'd exposed ourselves. Lord Vorkoth sent the other goblin clans after us. We would have been massacred. But we found out through our contacts among the Fae—because we'd been helping them we had friends among them—that the Fae Lords were leaving the Realm and taking as many of their people with them as they could. My clan found one of the gateways and passed through it just before it closed. We knew we couldn't assimilate into your world, so we hid in the park, then used our arts to alter it, make it a place where we could be safe. And to make it more like home."

My jaw fell open. "*You* created Shadowpark!"

"Well, not me. It was the work of the Great Shaman and those of his circle. But yes, we created what you call Shadowpark."

"Wow, that's …" I shook my head. "You know, it killed a bunch of Fae Knights."

"We may be against the Shadow, but our magic still comes from the same place other goblin magic comes from—dark dimensions and dark gods. The Park will defend itself, brutally. It sensed a threat to itself—to us—and it reacted. I … I'm sorry it hurt your friends."

I could hear the truth of her words in her voice. I nodded.

"Thanks," I said. I wished I had more ale left. "Things have changed out there, you know. Outside of the park. With the Fae's coming all the shifters, mages and other supes have come out of the closet. Out of the den. The world is changing. There are already a few goblins here and there. Your people might find a place."

"We have a place. And those other goblins still serve the Shadow. They're our enemies."

"So you mean to stay here forever?"

"Well, for now. But we do send some of our members out into your world. To make contacts in the underworld, where we can interact more freely, and to gather intelligence."

"That's what you were doing."

She inclined her head. "Yes."

"You're a spy!"

"If you like."

"Wow, I'm friends with a goblin spy." I grinned. "We're friends now, right? I mean, we're bonding and all. Next we can do each other's nails."

"You are not touching my nails, Jade." But I thought she was smiling, just faintly.

Leaning forward, I gave her a hug. She didn't return it, but she didn't punch me, either. I thought that was progress.

Pulling back, I said, "So you were acting the part of a thief to make contacts in the underworld."

"That's right. Although in order to play the part I've actually become a pretty good one."

"I noticed."

"When I learned that a Fae Lord wanted to hire a crew to go after a wizard's artifact, I did some digging. Soon I became convinced it was Nevos. My clan hates him and blames him for the war, for my kind having to leave the Fae Lands. I wasn't going to kill him. I was going to capture him and bring him here. So that he could face justice. In the Arena."

My belly churned. "The Arena?"

She grinned, and it was a terrifying sight. "That's right. You're just in time. He should be granted his trial at any moment."

"Trial?"

"By combat."

I slumped back. "You're going to feed him to a monster ..."

"He'll be given a sword. If he's innocent, he'll prevail. The gods will see to it."

"But if he's not?"

She only smiled wider. Blood coated her teeth.

Chapter 17

I had to hurry. Nevos was due to be executed in less than an hour.

My heart thumped crazily in my chest as I slipped through the ground of the goblin castle. Part of me wanted to let them just do it. Nevos probably deserved whatever he had coming. But I'd slept with him, and I couldn't deny that part of me even liked him. No, don't look at me like that. I hadn't fallen for him or anything. But I did like him at least enough to want him to live.

And there was the fact that only he could help me defeat Angela. I still wasn't sure what she was after, but I knew he did.

He was my only hope.

I crept through the grounds of the goblin castle, intent on reaching the jailhouse before it was too late. A patrol ambled by and I shrunk into the shadows near a wall. The goblins marched past, not seeing me.

Something large hissed behind me. I spun, breathless, to see a horrible face peering at me from a window—one of the huge lizards the goblins rode. I'd hidden along the wall of a stable. A forked tongue flickered out between long sharp teeth, and the giant snake-like eyes stared at me unblinking. Probably wondering if I was tasty.

Shaking it off, I pushed on, seeking shelter where I could. Noises grew louder in the direction of the arena. The goblins were gathering there, preparing for justice to be delivered. I could see them smiling and talking animatedly—the word had gone out about Nevos. The excitement for his brutal death was almost palpable.

Another group of green-skinned warriors filed by, and I huddled against some crates until they were gone.

At last I reached the jailhouse.

"Nevos," I whispered, approaching one barred window. Nothing. "Nevos," I whispered at another. A horned head leered at me, burping drunkenly. I moved on. "Nevos?"

"Jade?"

The voice was crisp. Ready.

Nevos's handsome face appeared at a barred window. I went to it. It was dark, but I still marveled at how much like Davril he looked, only with long, wavy black hair and lustrous green eyes.

I cocked my head in the direction of all the commotion. "Hear that? You're a star."

"Sounds like it. I can't wait to meet my audience."

"Trust me, you can."

He studied me. "I break you out, now you break me out, is that it?"

"Something like that." I made myself meet his eyes. "I need answers, though. This isn't just one favor for another. You'll owe me for this."

Slowly, he nodded. "The knob. You want to know about the knob."

"That's right. You tell me what I need to know and I'll let you out."

He smiled. "Let me out and I'll tell you what you need to know."

"That's not the deal. Talk first."

He spread his hands wide. "Make me."

I groaned. "Fine, I'll get you out. But if you don't talk once we're clear of this place I'll make sure you face whatever's waiting for you in that arena. I'll even let Hela buy me a beer when that monster comes out."

"It's a deal," he said. "Just get me out of this place."

Quickly I assembled my spellgredients. The cell was warded, as were the bars, but I was an old pro at disabling such things, and I had rendered the wards useless after only a minute of working on it.

Once that was done, Nevos's inhuman strength made short work of the bars themselves. He simply grabbed them and shoved them out. I danced back. He pulled himself through the window and dropped beside me.

"Thanks," he said, flashing a grin.

"Sure. Just remember—"

"I know, I know. We had a deal."

"*Have* a deal."

He didn't argue. He scanned the surrounds, looking for the best way through. I had already picked out the easiest route to the wall and pointed it out to him. He silently agreed, and together we cut through the camp. Cheers went up in the direction of the arena, but also roars. Monsters were either fighting each other or goblin gladiators, maybe some sort of warm-up act.

"Hate to miss the show," Nevos said softly. "I do love a good bout."

"Help yourself, ace. But you're the show."

"That is a problem," he admitted.

A patrol of goblins filed by, all of them drinking and grumbling, clearly annoyed to be missing the festivities. They were the last patrol between us and the castle wall. Nevos and I hunkered in the shadows until they passed, then found a set of stairs and ran up the wall. Immediately a goblin on duty turned at hearing us. His eyes bulged.

He barked something at us in goblin-ish and ripped out his sword. I was already prepared and blew some dust into his eyes. He swayed to the side and collapsed, instantly asleep. Before any other goblins could find us, Nevos and I found some vines growing up the outside of the wall and climbed down. Nevos grinned widely when our feet touched down.

"Your help has been most appreciated, Jade McClaren," he said.

"You're not shed of me yet."

"Oh, I know." He paused. "I can see why Davril likes you."

"Who says he does?"

"Come now, Jade. You know that Angela's spies have been spying on you closely, and she filled me in while you were … indisposed. You and Davril have grown very close. But I wonder … do you know who he really is?"

"Don't try to drive us apart, jerkwad."

"*Jerkwad?* Now the fire comes out! Only it can't, can it? Sorry, that was mean. And you admit that there *is* something between you two." His tone softened. "Listen, Jade. I'm sorry, but Davril and I … and women … There's a bitter history there."

"Tell it later. We've got to go."

"Fine, but you—"

Shocked cries of anger and horror rose up on the other side of the wall. The small hairs on the nape of my neck shot up.

"They've noticed your disappearing act," I said.

"Let's go."

A long, low horn blew, sending chills throughout my body, and the sound of the gate slamming open reached us. We ran and ducked through the nighttime forest, the rasps and growls of reptilian beasts not far behind us.

"They're riding their big lizards," I said.

"Golms," Nevos said, only panting slightly. "They're called golms. They ride them in the Fae Lands, too."

I ducked a branch, ran on. Roots tangled about my feet. I tripped but righted myself.

A goblin cried out behind us. I heard a whistling noise and jerked to the side just as a spear hurtled through the space I'd just been. It embedded in the trunk of a tree, quivering.

I ripped the spear loose, showering bark, spun and hurled the spear right into the chest of the goblin who had thrown it. He made a comical "Ack" sound and listed to the side, then fell out of the stirrups. *Sorry, Hela. I hope he wasn't a friend.* His golm ran on, but it seemed confused. Inspiration struck me.

"Can you summon your light?" I asked Nevos. "Blind the others?" A dozen riders were just behind the now-riderless golm, getting closer with every heartbeat.

Nevos nodded, seeing what I wanted. When we reached a few thick trees, he paused and turned, seeking shelter. A spear whistled by, then a hail of arrows. The stench of poison wafted off them. Nevos's jaw bulged in concentration and he thrust out his palms. Light gathered there, then flashed out in a blinding rush, sweeping over the goblins and their hideous mounts. The goblins shrieked and threw their hands over their eyes.

"Come!" I said.

I dashed out to the riderless golm and jumped into the saddle. Nevos followed suit, leaping on immediately behind me. His large arms went round my waist, and I liked the feel of his hard body behind me.

The light would only blind the goblins for a moment. I grabbed the reins, kicked the golm in the flanks and said, "Ra!" The goblins probably didn't use "ra", but the golm seemed to get the point and jumped forward. I guided it through the dark, dripping trees, in what I hoped was the shortest way out of Shadowpark.

"Good thinking," Nevos said.

"Thanks."

He kissed the back of my head. I didn't whip my head back and break his nose.

Goblins called out behind us, and soon I could hear the sounds of them and their golms coming after us again. They seemed to have lost us, though, and were trying to pick our trail up again. *Be fast,* I sent to the golm we were riding. *Be fast and true.*

We rode hard, my heart beating wildly, sweat drenching me, and with every breath I inhaled the scent of Nevos's adrenaline ... and pheromones. He clearly liked being pressed up against me, and I still wasn't trying to pummel him to death. *He's the enemy, Jadeslut. Focus!*

"This way," Nevos said, pointing. "I think this way is the shortest way out."

I turned the golm in the direction he'd indicated, hoping he wasn't leading me into a trap. But then, how could he? He'd lost everything, all his allies, one by one. And all in search of whatever the knob belonged to.

"Okay," I said. "It's time."

Amusement laced his voice. "Time?"

"Don't make me get this golm to eat you. You know what I'm talking about."

He laughed. "Don't worry, Jade. I'm a man of my word. The knob belongs to an ancient wardrobe once owned by an Earth-based High Priest of Lord Vorkoth."

"The Shadow was worshipped here ... on Earth?"

"That's right. And the High Priest could communicate directly with Lord Vorkoth himself ... through the wardrobe."

A stream ahead. I guided the golm to a shallow spot. Droplets splashed us as we crossed, but I barely felt them. The goblin hunters seemed far behind us.

"How could the Shadow communicate through a stupid wardrobe?" I said.

"I don't understand the magic involved, honestly. I think the laws that such energies obey shift over time. I'm not even sure that spell is possible anymore. Hence the reason why that wardrobe is so important. But what I do know is that the High Priest would simply open the wardrobe, and inside would be a great, living darkness, and it would speak with him."

"The Shadow."

"Exactly. The High Priest would carry out Lord Vorkoth's will here on Earth, and he had a large following. Agents of the Light eventually eradicated them all, and the wardrobe was thought lost for all time. It was damaged in the fighting, and one of the knobs was hewn off. That knob's location was traced throughout the years, sometimes surfacing in the hands of a collector, sometimes disappearing for decades."

"Who cares about the knob?"

"It has always been supposed that a powerful enough witch or wizard could use the knob to locate what it once belonged to. Was once a part of."

I nodded. "Like Ruby can use the lock of a person's hair to find the whole person."

"Right."

"So that's what this all has been about—finding the wardrobe."

"And being able to communicate with Lord Vorkoth. Yes." Nevos released a caged breath. "I knew where to begin looking for the knob, but I had no idea where the wardrobe was, although rumors say that it's somewhere in New York. But Angela cracked the knob's secrets last night—that is, her great working revealed the location of the wardrobe."

"Well? Are you going to tell me?"

He laughed again. He laughed a lot for someone who had just lost two friends and almost been thrown into a monster-filled pit.

"No," he said. "That wasn't part of the bargain."

"Bastard!"

"Don't feel bad. The truth is I don't really know. I stole the knob from Angela, but she never deigned to tell me what she'd learned from it—that is, where the wardrobe is."

"Then how are you planning to find it?"

"The working she performed on the knob is still fresh. If I can find a powerful enough witch or wizard, someone who can divine the nature of the working and tell me what Angela learned, I should be able to find the wardrobe on my own. Hopefully before she does."

"Then what?"

"Then I'll be in possession of the wardrobe. I'll be able to communicate with Lord Vorkoth directly."

"You mean you can't?"

He sighed. "Sadly, no. My lord can't bridge the gulf between dimensions. This world is locked off from him. Only something like the wardrobe, which was built before that locking-out happened, can enable an adherent of the Shadow to commune with Him. And when I have it, Angela's people will turn on her and support me."

"Why?"

"I have many agents amongst her camp, just as she was able to plant one of her people amongst my small crew. They've been spreading the word of my high placement in the Dark Lord's councils and how it would be better for them if I were in charge. If I can secure the wardrobe, they'll rise up and supplant Angela in favor of yours truly."

"So the fate of the world hinges on a wardrobe. I always knew clothes were important."

He chuckled. "Always."

Ahead of us the air darkened. We were nearing the Veil that separated Shadowpark from the real world—that is, the rest of New York.

"We made it," I said.

His arms tightened around my middle. For a moment I stiffened, afraid he was about to try to move against me. It made sense. After all, he'd just told me his plan. Now he would have to get rid of me—at least that's what I was thinking. But he only pulled me back against him and said, very softly, in my ear, "On the other side, we'll have to go our separate ways, Jade. Unless you want to join me."

"And serve the Shadow? Hell no."

"Then we'll be enemies the next time we meet."

We entered the Veil, and things grew murky and strange. Reality lurched and snapped all around us. Then we were through. Sunlight stabbed at my eyes, and I mashed them against it. I wasn't used to daylight after my sojourn in Shadowpark. Time passed differently in the park, and I tried to place the hour. Somewhere around noon, I thought.

A police patrol was just rounding the bend, passing out of sight, leaving Nevos and I riding a giant lizard near the ruined wall that had once enclosed Shadowpark before monsters and other baddies overran it a few years ago.

I swung down from the lizard and alit on the asphalt. It felt good to have good old-fashioned road under my feet. Putting my fingers to my lips, I whistled loudly, then again. Nevos arched his eyebrows.

I smiled as Chromecat appeared from above, her gorgeous black wings flapping. Engine purring, she flew down from the skies and landed on the road beside me.

"Good to see you, girl," I said, stroking her handlebars. To Nevos, I said, "You can keep the lizard."

Nevos patted the creature's flank. "There's a good lad." His face turned serious. "Jade ..."

I swallowed. "Yeah?"

"It was a pleasure getting to know you."

To my surprise, tears built behind my eyes. I didn't let them out. Life was wild, stranger than I ever would have supposed, but it was dangerous, too.

"You, too," I said.

He positioned himself into the golm's saddle and took the reins. He started to twitch them to guide the creature off, but hesitated.

"Jade?"

I slid onto Chromecat's seat and revved the motor. The engine throbbed pleasantly beneath me. "Yeah?" I called over the noise. Chromecat was smoother and quieter than a normal bike, but she still wasn't noiseless.

"There's something you should know about Davril," Nevos said.

Here it comes. I'd known Nevos had some ace up his sleeve, some way to try to turn me against Davril. Now he was about to show his hand.

"Lay it on me," I said. I tried to appear strong, but inside I braced myself.

"Ask him about Liana." Anger tinged his voice. "Ask him about my wife."

I blinked. "Your *wife?*"

He nodded, slowly, his face taut, his eyes like daggers. "I loved her dearly, but he seduced her behind my back. He stole her from me."

"Davril would *never* do that! He's noble and honorable, almost to a fault."

"He's lied to you, Jade. You don't know him like you think you do. He's not the man you think he is."

"Oh, but you are?"

He regarded me in silence, and there was heat in his features. *Damn*, I realized. He *liked* me. Shit! Life really *was* complicated, wasn't it?

"You could do worse," he said quietly.

I stood my ground. "You're lying. Davril would never betray you like that."

"It's the truth, Jade. He's a deceiver. Do you think I turned against the Fae on a whim? I would never. I had no honorable course other than what I did. He betrayed me. Stole my wife. And then …"

I held my breath. "What?"

His eyes grew misty. "She died."

Grief welled up in me, not just because of his words but because of the obvious emotion in him. It wracked his soul, I could tell. Despite everything, he still loved Liana. And he hated Davril. But I couldn't believe it. The picture he painted just wasn't the Davril that I knew.

"You're lying," I said.

His shook his head, once, brusquely, confidently. "No, Jade. I'm not." He paused. "Are you sure you want to return to him? You can't win against me. I *will* have that wardrobe. I *will* be able to commune with Lord Vorkoth. And once that happens, how can you stand against me? Come with me, Jade. Reign at my side. We will bring this world to its knees, and the Shadow will rule over us. But we will have dominion over this realm. As King and Queen of the Earth."

I stared at him. Wind howled, and the noise of Chromecat's engine seemed very far away. All there was in the entire world was Nevos and me, and his terrible, wonderful offer.

At last I shook myself.

"Never," I said. "And you won't have that wardrobe, either."

One corner of his mouth pulled up. "But I will, Jade. I've got the knob. I've got it right …" His hand patted his pocket, right where the knob had been. He patted it, but there was nothing there. Shock, then anger filled his features. "Jade, what have you done?"

I laughed and patted my own pocket, where I could feel the bulge of the knob against my fingers.

"I'm saving the world," I said.

I gunned the engine and roared down the street. Chromecat's black wings stretched to either side, stroking the air. Nevos shouted and cursed behind me, but I grinned and lifted off, taking to the skies once more. I was free, and I had the knob. *Angela, watch out.*

Chapter 18

My mind churned as I flew along. Wind whipped my hair behind me, and my body took that moment to remember all my aches and pains and exhaustion. But my mind couldn't let go of Nevos's words.

Could Davril really have betrayed him and seduced his wife, thus leading to Nevos's own dark turn and the fall of the Fae? It couldn't be, I told myself. It just couldn't be.

But there had been truth in Nevos's face. There had been honesty there. I didn't know what to believe.

Tormented, I flew on.

What I *did* know was that I needed to bring the knob to a powerful witch and to have her divine the nature of Angela's working upon it. Do that and we could find the wardrobe. We could get to it before she did and stop her from forging a direct link to the Shadow. I didn't know what exactly that kind of link could accomplish, but I doubted it would be a good thing.

I headed straight for Ruby's place. *Our* place. For some reason I was thinking of it more and more as her place, I don't know why.

About halfway there I noticed movement behind me and glanced over my shoulder.

"Shit."

The bird of fire was behind me—the same creature that had pursued me and Ruby after leaving the Guild of Thieves. Flames rising from its wings, the huge creature was descending from the clouds, where it had been lurking. It shrieked and dove toward me.

My blood ran cold.

I jerked the handlebars, aiming the bike at a building. My hairs stood on end. I could feel the bird behind me. Gritting my teeth, I swerved around the corner of the building. The bird swept past.

I aimed at another building and made a curve. Glancing over my shoulder, I could no longer see the creature. Shaking, I continued on toward Ruby, hoping and praying I had lost the thing. I deepened the shadows around me, but I wasn't sure if those even worked against this thing. If nothing else, I couldn't see it anymore.

I was still tense and on edge when I reached the apartment building and hitched Chromecat to the terrace balcony, then made it invisible.

Ruby was watching a B horror movie in the living room when I entered, but she hadn't seemed to be paying it much attention. Her eyes were red and her hair and clothes disheveled. She leapt up with a cry when she saw me and wrapped me in a crushing hug.

"Jade!" she said, sobbing. "Thank God you're back! I was so worried about you."

I laughed and hugged her back, tight. My eyes burned and I may have cried a little. Chest hitching, I said, "I was worried about myself."

She wiped her eyes and pulled back. She studied me, shaking her head. "What the hell, sis? What happened to you? You look terrible."

I let out a breath. "I need a drink."

"First you need the healing stone."

She took me into her room and made me hold the healing stone in my hands, then said a spell to activate it. The stone only worked once a month, or at least it took a month to regenerate its powers after a usage, so I knew I must have been in pretty bad shape for Ruby to waste a round on me. It worked, though. My cuts and bruises and whip-lashes began to heal, and I felt lighter and clearer. Afterward, we moved to the kitchen. She poured us both a shot of whiskey, then another. Over shots and sips, and I told my tale, relating all that had happened to me in Shadowpark—yep, even what happened between me and Nevos in his bedroom. Her eyes grew huge.

"I can't believe it," she said.

"Yep. It was really that big."

"Not about that!" She swatted my shoulder. "About everything. Do you really believe Davril betrayed his brother?"

I was silent, then: "I hope not."

"But you think he might have."

"I … don't know."

She was silent a long time, then finally said, "And you still have it?"

With all the drama I could muster, I drew the knob from my pants pocket and placed it on the table. Ruby gazed at it, then reached out a hand to sense it without touching it. Satisfied, she picked it up and brought it close to her eyes, taking in every grain and chip of wood.

"This thing could lead to the Wardrobe of Doom, huh?"

"Apparently. You think you can hack Angie's spell or whatever and locate the rest of the dresser?"

"I … think so. But it will take some time."

"Good. I'm beat. I need some shut eye." The bed in the goblin keep hadn't allowed me the deep rest my body craved, and the healing stone had left me drowsy.

She nodded. "You've earned it. But …"

"Yeah?"

"Don't you think you should call Davril first?"

I frowned. I'd been wondering the same thing. I hadn't come up with any answers, though. I was still trying to puzzle out my response to Nevos's claims. What I *should* feel and what I *did* feel. I didn't trust Nevos further than I could throw him, but I didn't think he'd been lying, either. So did that mean Davril had lied to *me?*

I yawned. "I'll call him when I wake up."

I marched to my bedroom and flung myself on the bed. I was asleep before my head hit the pillow. My dreams were wild and restless, and I kept seeing Nevos's face flashing before me, replaced by Davril's. Then Angela would appear, laughing manically and wielding her whip of fire. And in the background loomed the wardrobe, huge and dark, pregnant with dark possibilities. At last, gasping, I lurched up in bed, fully awake.

Davril set on the foot of the bed.

"Davril!"

He smiled gently. "Jade."

For a small eternity, we stared at each other. My heart beat like a drum, and sweat stung my eyes. I knew I must have been tossing and turning, moaning and sweating. The sheets were everywhere.

I wasn't sure who was going to speak first, but then he said, "I was worried about you. Thank the gods you're all right."

That put a little spark back in me. "You were worried about me?"

Then I remembered I was mad at him. I sagged.

"What is it?" he said.

I'd lowered my gaze, tilting my face downward, but now I looked at him out of my downturned face. "I met Nevos," I said quietly.

"Ruby told me."

"Did she call you?"

"No. I …" He grimaced. "I hope you don't mind, but I had someone watching your place to alert me when you returned." He hastened to add, "I've never done it before, don't worry, and won't again, but I … well, I needed to know you were safe. And it's important, too. Important to my people, and yours."

"Did Ruby tell you what happened?"

"Not in detail, no, but I saw her working on the knob, and she told me what it was."

I nodded raggedly. "I guess it's time to debrief you. Let me brush my teeth first."

I went to the bathroom and let him wait for awhile. While I was in there, I tried to get myself together, but it wasn't happening. I was a mess. Until I could get this thing resolved, it was going to eat me up. But how did you start that conversation? *Hey Davril, so I heard you betrayed your brother and ushered in the downfall of your people? Pass the salt.* I stared at myself in the mirror and sighed.

Davril was inspecting the various items littering our apartment—ancient swords on the walls, a suit of armor, a Chinese fan. All prize pieces of loot gained through our lives of crime. Each was important to Ruby and me.

He raised his eyebrows at me and stood straighter, turning his attention from the crystal wand on its pedestal. "You look better," he said.

I narrowed my eyes at him, trying to be playful. "Thanks."

He studied me. "Jade …"

"Yes?"

My heart went bump-thump, bump-thump.

He opened his mouth to say something. Just then Ruby came down the hallway. She saw us, looked at our faces, made a panicked expression and scurried away. I wished I could go with her. Yep, this was the serious drama time. I hated drama.

"Jade," Davril said slowly, coming closer. He reached out a hand and touched mine. Normally the gesture would have thrilled me. Unable to help it, though, I pulled my hand back. A flicker of pain passed across Davril's usually stoic face.

"I … I'm sorry," I said.

"What is it? Clearly something's bothering you." When I didn't say anything, he frowned. "Is it Nevos?"

"I need a drink."

I wasn't sure how long I'd slept, but it was dark outside and I was hungry. My thirst was even greater. I rummaged through the fridge, found a good pale ale, popped the top and downed a long, cold, foamy sip.

"Ah," I said. "That's better. Washes out the toothpaste taste. Do Fae use toothpaste?"

"Jade, what is going on with you?" Davril had followed me into the kitchen but hadn't made a move to find a drink of his own.

You're going to need it, I thought.

I peered down the hall, making sure Ruby wasn't listening in (although how could you tell with a witch?), then said, "Well … I mean …"

"Yes?"

He looked at me with innocent, sincere, deeply blue and majestic eyes. I could fall right into those things and drown in bliss. Well, if I weren't in the mood I was in, that was. Right now I just wanted to poke him in the eyes like Mo of the Three Stooges always used to do to Larry and Curly. Boomp!

I took another long slurp.

Just spit it out, Jade! But where did I start? Did I start with the part where I'd betrayed Davril with Nevos, or where I suspected Davril had betrayed his brother with

Liana? I mean, if we were both betrayers, what did it even matter? Maybe we deserved each other.

But I'd only done it so I could get close to the knob and steal it back. Why had Davril done it?

If he had?

Davril approached me, a tender but perplexed look on his face. "Jade, I'm here for you. Whatever happened, I need to know. I'll help you through it, whatever it is."

A spike of anger pulsed behind my eyes. "Yeah, and did you help Nevos's wife through whatever was bothering her?"

He blinked and his head jerked back, as if I'd slapped him. "W-what did you say?"

"Ha! I've never heard you stammer before. Caught you out, didn't I?" For some reason the evidence of his guilt made me feel more righteous about confronting him.

"I … I …" He passed a hand across his face and slumped back against the wall. I watched the play of subtle emotions cross his face, and for a moment it was I who felt guilty.

"I think I will take that drink," he said.

He moved to the refrigerator and snagged a cold one. He normally didn't drink beer, so this must be big. I mean, the bottle of wine was just sitting right there on the counter, and I knew he preferred wine. But if he couldn't even take the time to find a glass and pour, then I knew Nevos must have been telling the truth, or some version of it.

Damn.

When he'd taken a long sip, Davril turned back around. His eyes moved to me, then moved on, and I knew he was seeing another place, another time.

"Liana …"

His voice was hoarse, almost a whisper. The pain in it was so clear that I almost started to cry. Just the memory of Liana was enough to cause him distress. The question was whether he deserved it. That was something I meant to find out. If my own partner would betray his brother, why wouldn't he betray me, too?

Part of me shrank in fear. Because sooner or later Davril would find out that I'd slept with Nevos, and he might think that constituted a betrayal, as well. Even though it wasn't. At all. It hadn't meant anything. It was just part of the job. A very sexy, satisfying part of the job.

"Well?" I said at last. I didn't say it meanly, though. The anger had gone out of me, at least for the moment. I tried to say it strongly, but also with some sympathy. "Was she Nevos's wife?"

Slowly, he nodded. He took a long sip. "It was years ago," he said, his voice dreamy. "Before the fall of the Nine Thrones ... back when I sat one of those thrones myself."

"You were king."

Another sip. "Yes."

Slowly, as if locked in a trance, he pulled up a chair and sat down. When he didn't go on, I said, "You were a king, and you slept with your brother's wife. He found out, grew furious and turned on you. His anger was so great he even sided with the Shadow against you. Is that about right?" Despite my best efforts, anger was creeping back into my voice.

Davril said nothing, just stared at the wall, or through it, as if gazing into the past.

"That one act brought all this about," I said, waving the hand that wasn't holding my beer. "The collapse of your empire, the war, the flight from your homeland, the battles we've fought, are *still* fighting ..."

Distantly, mechanically, he said, "Yes."

That was it. No denial, no excuses, no explanations. I stared at him. I wanted to drag the excuses out of him. I knew there had to be more than that. There had to be. He was Davril Stormguard, damn it, knight and lord, noble and true. The man I loved.

Shit. Did I just think that? Take it back, I told myself. But it was too late.

I loved him. I knew that now. But if he was really to blame for all this, and there weren't any mitigating circumstances …

I pulled up a chair and sat next to him. "Davril," I said softly. "Tell me the truth. Tell me the story. I know you. I know you wouldn't just …"

Slowly, very slowly, his faraway eyes turned to me. "Jade, it's true. All of it. Liana died. Because of me."

My stomach churned. "How?"

"I …" He sighed and took a long pull. "I don't know where to begin, Jade. Nevos has a right to his anger. He's wrong, but he's also right."

"I don't know what any of that means, Dav. Walk me through it. Treat me like I'm not from the Fae Lands and don't know what you're talking about."

Before he could answer, someone knocked on the door. Both our heads snapped in that direction. The front door was just off the kitchen, and we could both see it.

"Were you expecting company?" Davril said.

"No." Raising my voice, I said, "Rubes, did you order a pizza or something?"

Silence, then Ruby appeared. She looked drained from using her magic, and I remembered her coming to find me minutes ago. Did that mean she had something to report? Had she found the location of the wardrobe?

There was no time to ask that now.

"No," she said. Her face was unusually tight, her eyes fixed on the door. "But I sense something …" She reached out a hand toward the door, questing. She gasped and dropped her hand. "Something powerful!"

Icy fingers traced down my spine.

The knocking came again, louder this time. I jumped.

Davril's hand moved to his hip, prepared to draw his sometimes invisible sword if necessary.

Swallowing, I moved to the door. I would open it, and Davril and Ruby would be braced to deal with whatever was on the other side. Before I could get there, however, the door exploded open with such force that I was hurled backward. I crashed into Ruby and we both went down flailing.

Cursing, I climbed back to my feet to find Davril on the ground, too. The air was filled with dust, and the kitchen table lay in splinters. The door sagged in its frame.

Davril climbed to his feet and whipped out his sword. It glowed palely in the dust-filled chamber. Then, slowly, the dust cleared, and revealed in the doorway was none other than Vincent Walsh.

"I believe you have something of mine," he said.

Chapter 19

I stared, hardly able to believe it. The world seemed to spin and shift around me. Vincent Walsh, my arch-nemesis, *here?* In my *home?* We had taken great pains to keep our place of residence concealed from enemies.

I found my voice. "Get the fuck out of here, you bastard!"

Unconsciously my gaze went to his left hand. There on his third finger glittered the black ring—the ring I had longed to get my hands on for years. Only without him around to fight me for it. Inside that ring was my fire. The missing piece of myself.

Tall and elegantly dressed, with dark hair and eyes, Walsh watched us smugly. Power radiated off him. At any moment he could become a dragon or use his magic to destroy us.

Well, he could try.

"Do your worst," Ruby said, coming to stand beside me.

Davril slashed his sword through the air, stalking forward. "You are not welcome here, monster."

Walsh narrowed his eyes. He was a handsome man, but there was so much malice and arrogance in his face that it robbed him of all attractiveness. He was loathsome and terrifying. When he narrowed his eyes, flames burned in the back of them. A bit of smoke curled up from his nostrils.

Davril paused. Wise man.

Walsh's gaze landed on me. His voice cracked like thunder: "Thief!"

I held my ground. "Look who's talking."

"Give me back what you stole."

"I will if you will." I indicated his ring.

His eyes smoldered. Literally. "All dragonfire shall be mine, you unworthy wretch. Now give me back what you stole and I might let you live."

"Gee, that sounds like such a sweet deal," Ruby said. One of her hands was in a fist, and I knew that the knob must be inside.

Walsh apparently figured that out, too. He raised the hand that didn't have the black ring on it, palm out toward Ruby. Her fist shook, then her arm, and her arm shot straight up, the knob inside her fist being drawn toward Walsh like a magnet.

Davril lunged at Walsh, sword flashing. Walsh simply opened his mouth and a blast of hot air sent Davril reeling backward, hair flying, skin turning red. I used the distraction to leap at the evil mage. He merely flicked the fingers of the hand that did bear the ring and suddenly I was floating through the void of space. Darkness whizzed around me, and stars. Then I was back in the kitchen, but on the far side of it, and frost had gathered in the fine hairs all over my body.

Whoa.

Ruby let out a cry and the knob flew through the air and landed in Walsh's waiting hand. Victory crossed his features as he regarded it.

"Bastard," I said.

His lips twitched upward. Slowly, though, his expression changed. Grew troubled.

"A working has been wrought upon it," he said. "The location of the wardrobe is known." Fury replaced the look of victory. "You fools, what have you done?"

Davril, Ruby and I glanced at each other, then back to Walsh. I was the first one to speak:

"What do you mean?"

Practically biting off the words, he said, "Why would you want the wardrobe? What possible use can it have for you?"

"We don't want it," Davril said, exploringly. "It was taken by a witch named Angela. Do you know her?"

Walsh stroked his chin. "Yes, I know her. A foul thing, seduced by the dark powers."

"Unlike you," I said.

Hastily, before Walsh could rebuke me, Ruby said, "What's this all about?"

Walsh paused. Behind him in the hallway I could hear people talking and doors opening and closing as people checked out the situation. They'd heard the exploding door and wanted to know what was going on. Of course, this being Gypsy Land it was even odds on whether they'd call the police. Just the same …

"If we're not going to kill each other, can we at least come inside?" I said.

Walsh stepped past the threshold. He snapped his fingers again and the splintered remains of the door resolidified, becoming a door once again.

"Wow," said Ruby. "You've got some major mojo."

I wanted to remind her that this bastard had killed our father and grandmother, but I didn't bother. I knew she hadn't let herself forget. Walsh may be evil, but his power *was* impressive.

Now that we weren't quite so conspicuous, I said, "Well? Are you going to tell us or leave us guessing?"

Walsh sneered. He shoved the knob away in a fold of his clothes. "You fools don't know what you've done. You've allowed a high servant of the Shadow to find a means of communing with him directly. This situation must be rectified." He considered us. "I suppose you could be useful. It would be better not to kill you. For now." He seemed to be speaking as much to himself as to us.

"What do you intend to do?" Davril demanded. He had his sword raised and seemed coiled for another lunge. I admired his bravery. It was all I could do not to turn around and run away.

"I intend to find that witch and stop her," Walsh said. "Before she can seize the wardrobe for herself. Its location had always eluded my spells, but Angela, using magic from a different set of dimensions, seems to have found her quarry. There may still be time, while her imprint is fresh upon this knob, to recreate her spell—"

"Already done it," Ruby said.

Walsh's eyebrows shot up. "You? Really?"

"Really."

"Where is it?" I asked her. "The wardrobe? Please don't tell me it's in Beijing or something."

"No." She shook her head, red hair swaying to either side. "It's right here in New York. In fact, it's somewhere you were at just yesterday."

I smacked my mouth. "You mean ..."

"That's right. It's at the Guild of Thieves."

"You're kidding me." Then again, it made a certain amount of sense. The Guild House had been cluttered with all sorts of magical items looted from a thousand different places. Grimacing, I added, "This should be interesting. I doubt Gavin is my biggest fan at the moment. That is, if Hela reported what happened between us."

Davril sheathed his sword, and I immediately missed its brightness. To Walsh, he said, "So. Are we allied, for the moment?"

Walsh inclined his head. "We have an agreement. Until the wardrobe is secured or destroyed, we shall work to thwart Angela and her minions. But I will not forgive your trespass upon my property, nor your burglary. And I know that you seek my death in some misguided quest for revenge, Jade McClaren. In self defense I must end you—if not today, then some day."

I suppressed a shudder. "Let's make tracks."

*　　*　　*

I could only vaguely appreciate the beauty of the city as it scrolled by below us. All four of us rode in Lady Kay, with Chromecat following immediately behind. I wasn't sure how Walsh had arrived at our apartment and he didn't volunteer the information. Maybe he'd simply teleported there. I wouldn't put it past him. Either way, he seemed content to ride with us to the Guild House. He and Ruby rode in back, me and Davril in front. Davril, of course, drove.

"This is nuts," I whispered to him. I didn't think Walsh could hear us over the sounds of the wind and the city, but I spoke extra softly to be sure.

Davril just nodded. He drove on, silent and grim.

"I guess we'll have to resume our conversation another time," I said.

He nodded tightly. Both of us knew now wasn't the time, but our conversation from earlier was important. The truth about what had happened between Davril and Nevos needed to come out or there could be no trust between us.

I couldn't believe this was happening. Vincent Walsh, my arch-enemy, riding in the backseat! My skin crawled just to be so close to him. I pitied Ruby for having to sit next to him. I couldn't have done it. I would have started screaming. *Fuck* that guy.

I sucked in a deep breath, steadying myself.

With all the courage I could summon, I turned in my seat and met Walsh's gaze. "How did you find us?" I said. When he didn't answer immediately, I added, "It was the bird, wasn't it? The bird of fire."

"It is a construct of mine. I'd given it to some of my ... associates."

"The vampires!" I said. "The vampire women at the Guild of Thieves. They work for you, right? When they saw me and Ruby, they sent that fire bird to track us."

"Perhaps it was something like that," Walsh allowed. "After I had chased you into Shadowpark, I set the construct to monitor it for your return to the outside world. It tracked you to your lair and there I confronted you. Satisfied?"

"Why are you so hot for the knob, anyway?" Ruby said. Then giggled. Of course.

Davril's hands twisted the wheel, and there was an edge to his voice. "Yes, wizard, I would hear this, too. Why were you so set on retrieving this item?"

Walsh sniffed. "Clearly to keep fools like Angela from finding the wardrobe and establishing a direct connection to the Shadow."

"Why do *you* care?" I snapped. "You're as bad as he is!"

Walsh fixed me with a heavy-lidded reptilian gaze. "If that were true, my dear, would you not all be dead by now?"

"Go on," Davril said, speaking through gritted teeth. "Threaten her again. I dare you."

Walsh grinned at us nastily but didn't push the issue.

"Wait," said Ruby. "Are you an *enemy* of the Shadow?"

Walsh drew himself up, aloof and remote. "My quest is my own private affair."

"Fuck that," I said. "You've tried to roast me several times over it, using what might be my own fucking fire. Fuck you. You've involved me in this. It's not private anymore."

"You involved yourself," he said, anger seeping into his tone. "You trespassed in my domicile. Stole my property."

"Which you no doubt stole from someone else, probably killing them in the process. You don't get to lecture me on morals, asshole." It was all I could do not to throw myself over the seat and strangle him. I knew the effort would probably get me killed, but I couldn't help it. My whole body shook with the effort of holding myself back.

Davril seemed to sense it. Slowly, calmly, he said, "Jade."

"Mm?"

"Get ready. We're almost there."

I spared Walsh another angry glare, then faced front again and sat back down. I crossed my arms across my chest.

"Thank you," Davril said. He hit a few buttons on the console.

"Dispatch," said a voice.

"This is Lord Stormguard," said Davril. "Summon the Order of the Shield to arms. Have them rallied and ready to attack in twenty minutes."

There came a pause. Then, slightly nervously: "Yes, sir. Are you coming here to lead them, or should I send them to a location?"

"Have them ready to assault the Guild of Thieves on my command."

He gave her the address, and she said, "Yes, sir. I'll get right on it."

He switched off and leaned back, looking reassured. I would have smiled, but I just couldn't, not with that assmaggot in the back seat. Still, it was pretty awesome to be able to call in an army of Fae Knights when you needed it. Davril flew Lady Kay downtown, right toward the Guild of Thieves, then brought Lady Kay in for a landing. She became invisible as we grew closer to the street, and we jumped down to the side walk the passers-by barely even noticed—all part of her magic.

The Guild House loomed, dark and encrusted with gargoyles, black columns lining its façade. It looked properly mysterious and forbidding, a den of vice and dark magic.

"I don't get it," Ruby said. "Why do they even have the wardrobe?"

"They probably don't even know what it is," I said. "They have a lot of crap in there."

Walsh flexed his fingers, and power snapped between them. "Let's get this over with. I don't enjoy your company enough to prolong this."

"I think the feeling's mutual," Davril said.

Pleasantries out of the way, we marched across the street and up the dark steps leading into the guild building. I pounded on the huge door, remembering Ruby's and my first visit here. I doubted this one was going to go much better, but there was always hope. If we could destroy the wardrobe, maybe Angela would just give up and go home.

"What's in the wardrobe, anyway?" Ruby said, twirling a strand of hair in her fingers.

"The Shadow," Walsh said ominously.

She frowned at him. "No, I mean are there any clothes in it? Is it empty? I mean, other than Mr. Darkface, or whatever?"

"It is filled with a howling darkness, you fool. A direct connection across dimensions to the one and only Lord Vorkoth."

"Oh. I only thought it might have some clothes, too."

No one was coming to the door. I knocked again. Davril nudged me, indicating something behind us. I turned but didn't see anything, just various people coming and going down the street. Typical New York. Only … wait … not everyone was coming and going, were they? Some were stopped, just standing there on the sidewalks, their faces pointed toward the guild building. Most were rough types, like bikers, but there were some fancifully dressed men and women that might be mages.

I swore. "Angela's army."

"Looks like she's readying her forces to strike," Davril agreed.

"Great."

"All the more reason to finish this quickly," Walsh said. Looking annoyed, he said, "Well, since they're answering your summons …"

He stretched out a fist and smashed it on the huge doors. A great BOOM rolled outward, startling me and everyone in the vicinity. Ruby stuck a finger in her ear.

"Damn," I said. "Give us a heads up next time you're going to do that."

"I did."

It worked. The grand doors swung inward, revealing the grandiose foyer with its broad tile floor and curling staircase. Cautiously, we stepped across the threshold. The door slammed shut behind us, making me jump once more. I was really on edge.

Dark figures rose up around us, oozing up out of the floor like liquid smoke. Their eyes burned, and their long gangly arms ended in wicked claws. The things weren't shadowmen, but they were similar, and they stank like rancid oil. I gasped and yanked out my crossbow, one of my backups that I'd retrieved from the apartment. Davril's sword slashed the air, and he cried out, "Come no closer!" Ruby crouched, her hands raised, ready to cast some spell.

Only Walsh looked unperturbed. He stood, calm and cool as a statue. The man was a reptile.

The dark figures parted, and a slim, dapper figure stepped forward.

"Gavin!" I said. My crossbow centered on his chest.

"Manners, manners," he said. His red goatee quivered as he spoke.

Reluctantly, I lowered the crossbow. I spared a nervous glance at the shadow-things, then jerked my gaze back to Gavin.

"What the hell?" I said.

"You and Ruby are welcome here, Jade. But you are not permitted to bring friends with you. Especially not a Fae Knight and a … whatever you are." He said this last scowling at Walsh.

Walsh's lips curved up, but the smile didn't reach his eyes. They were as cold and remote as ever. "I am a mage."

There's the simplification of a lifetime, I thought.

To Gavin, I said, "Sorry about that, G-man. But you're going to be glad I brought them. The witch called Mistress Angela is gathering an army outside, and I'm afraid she's going to strike at any moment." I made go-away motions at the shadow-monsters. "Can you get them to back the hell off?"

Gavin was hardly listening to this last part. "An army? What for?"

I gestured again at the shadows. "Them first."

He sighed and clapped his hands. The shadows retreated, but they didn't fade. At least I and the others had a little room to breathe.

"You're the Minister of the Guild?" Davril said.

"That's right. And I don't appreciate self-righteous Fae Lords entering my place of business. But I must see if what you say is true …"

Without another word, he stalked toward the staircase, and his shadows were swept up in his wake. Ruby and I glanced at each other, shrugged and followed. Davril, then Walsh trailed behind us. Davril looked to either side and up and down with every step, clearly certain that something terrible was about to pounce on us at any moment. And it probably was. Walsh, the murderous horror, feared nothing. Except, evidently, the Shadow. Which was *very* interesting.

Gavin marched up the stairs and then around the landing to a bank of high windows overlooking the street. Careful to keep our distance from his shadow warriors, the others and I massed at the window, too. Sure enough, more of Angela's goons had joined those already there. Grim, hard faces peered up from the street, staring straight at us. Malice and determination showed in them. Just seeing them made me feel cold.

Gavin muttered something under his breath and stood straighter, as if forcing himself to be brave. His expression was troubled.

"We're under siege," he said.

Chapter 20

"Don't worry," Davril told Gavin. "My people are gathering even now to fend Angela's soldiers off."

Gavin sniffed. "You think I want your help?"

Davril narrowed his eyes. "Don't think that I want to give it, but it is our duty, to defend even the likes of you."

"Hey," I said. "Gavin and I have more than a few things in common."

Davril didn't apologize. At least he didn't keep going with his tirade. Gavin and I had that in common, too: Fae righteousness could really get on your nerves.

Speaking in clipped words, the Guild Minister said, "What are they here for, the soldiers? What is this all about?"

"The wardrobe," Walsh said. "They seek the wardrobe."

"Wardrobe? I know of no wardrobe … not that would hold special significance, anyway."

"So you *do* know of a wardrobe?" Ruby said.

"Well … yes …" Gavin ran his hands down his velvet suit. "I need something to keep my attire in, don't I?"

Ruby smiled. "I knew it! There *are* clothes." Her face fell. "Too bad they're a guy's clothes."

"A stylish guy," I amended, and she nodded.

"Yeah. Gavin is a clotheshorse, isn't he?"

"Show us the wardrobe," Davril said, all business.

Gavin shrugged and led the way through high dark halls toward what might be his bedchamber. The air was cool, but my blood burned hot. His shadow warriors faded as we went, so at least there was that. Gavin had decided that we weren't the real threat.

"By the way, Jade," he said. "What happened on the job I sent you on? I never heard back from either Hela or the client, but I *have* heard from the others in your crew requesting payment."

That was a load off. Hela hadn't bothered informing on me before lighting out for Shadowpark.

I hitched my thumb at Walsh. "Gavin, meet the asshat we stole the item from."

Gavin looked stricken. *"What?"* For a moment he wavered, but he managed to keep going.

"Tell him," I told Walsh. "Did we steal the item from you or not?"

Walsh patted a pocket, where he must have tucked the knob away. "You did indeed."

"There!" I told Gavin. "You better pay up."

"But I got it back," Walsh added.

"Maybe with a penalty," I told Gavin. "Like, you pay eighty percent or something."

Gavin's brows drew together. "I won't pay out unless you completed the job and handed the item off to the client."

"Ah, well we did that, too. Only this asshat showed up later."

"Stop calling me that," Walsh growled.

"I'm sorry, but unless the client gives me the okay, I can't pay out," Gavin said.

"That's what I get for joining things," I said. "Bureaucracy and red tape."

We passed rooms and side halls, and occasionally people, too. Gavin wasn't the sole inhabitant of this place. Some were dressed in suits and dresses, some in leather and sequins. Probably some were employees or functionaries of the Guild, while others were fellow thieves. I looked for Walsh's vampires but didn't see them. Not that he needed any help. Bastard could turn into a gigantic red dragon anytime he wanted. At last Gavin led us to a large oaken door. He waved his hands over some runes and muttered words I couldn't make out, and the door swung open.

"I don't normally let strangers into my private rooms," he said. "But I'll put this down as a special occasion."

He ushered us into his lavish suite, with expensive carpets, elaborately wrought candelabras blazing purple lights, and mirrors hanging from nearly every wall.

"Damn," Ruby said. "You sure do like to look at yourself, don't you?"

Gavin glanced at himself in a mirror we were passing, seemed to see something amiss and dusted off some imaginary lint. "Well, I do have an image to maintain."

"Enough conversation," Davril said. "Where's the wardrobe?"

Gavin showed us into a huge, sumptuous bedroom. A massive four-poster bed dominated it. A mirror hung on the ceiling above—big surprise. The room was gigantic, and it had room for not just the bed and other trappings, like the couch and chairs and incense holders, but also a grandiose wardrobe against the wall opposite the bed. Huge and dark, with curlicues at the edges and clawed feet holding it up, the thing loomed gigantically. And sure enough, the knob on its left door, if you looked very closely, was a slightly different color than the other one. You really had to squint to see it, but that's the first thing my eyes went to, and I could tell the difference. A casual observer wouldn't have even known to look, though, and I doubted it had ever given Gavin pause.

"That's it," Walsh said immediately. He was staring with reptilian intensity at the item of furniture.

"I really don't see what the big deal is," Ruby said. "And it's waaaay too gothic. I mean, tone it down a notch, right? Whatever happened to subtlety?"

I turned to Davril. "Can you sense anything?"

"You mean, like the Shadow?" he said. "No, but I can feel great power. Great ... potential."

Wearing a perplexed expression, Gavin approached the wardrobe and flung it open.

"No!" Ruby said, and coiled for battle.

But instead of a swirling, howling darkness, only a rack of clothes and some drawers greeted us. The clothes *were* spiffy, though.

"Nice," I told Gavin.

He preened. "I do try."

Davril turned to Walsh. "Do it."

Walsh raised his eyebrows, either questioning Davril's meaning or questioning Davril's right to command him.

"Burn it," Davril clarified.

"Don't presume to give me orders," Walsh said. "But very well, that time has come, and there's no use delaying."

"*Burn* it?" Gavin said. Panicked, he threw his arms wide, shielding the wardrobe with his body. "You know what I paid for this thing? Well," he amended, "okay, technically I didn't pay anything. It was stolen by an associate some years ago from a wizard's manse, and I liked it so much I kept it for myself. But I could have sold it and made a tidy sum, and I didn't. I think that counts as paying for it." He cleared his throat and made his voice as commanding as he could. "You are *not* destroying my damned wardrobe."

"Out of the way," Walsh said.

"Hang on," Ruby said. "At least let him get his clothes out."

"This is an outrage!" Gavin said. "Jade, if you let this happen I will expel you from the Guild! How dare you!"

I let out a breath. "I know, Gav. It sucks. But you saw that army out there? They want this wardrobe, and they've got bad plans for it. And I don't mean disco."

His face fell. "Fine. I see you mean to do it whether I agree or not." With obvious reluctance, he stepped aside …

… and two dark figures materialized behind him. At first I thought they were his shadow warriors, but then I saw the long ratty hair on each one, the shapeless gray robes and the empty eye sockets that were really black wells plunging into endless darkness.

"Angela's witches!" I said.

One grabbed Gavin around the torso with one arm and stuck a gleaming dagger against his throat with her free hand. The other raised a gnarled wand at the rest of us.

"W-where did you come from?" Gavin demanded. "The wards on the Guild House are impenetrable!"

The eyeless witches hissed and screeched. I resisted the urge to fling my hands over my ears.

"We followed them in," hissed the one holding her wand up, indicating us.

"Fuck a duck," said Ruby.

"Language," I said, but my mind was spinning. This was all going terribly wrong.

"We will take the wardrobe," said the other eyeless witch. "You will all stand aside or suffer."

Instead of standing aside, Walsh stepped toward them. He opened his mouth and fire gushed out, shooting through the air toward the witches—and Gavin. He obviously didn't care if he roasted the Minister.

The witch holding the wand simply flicked her wrist. An energy shield shimmered into being in front of them. The flame hit it, bounced back, and rushed directly toward Walsh and the rest of us.

Ruby dove one way, and Davril and I dove the other. When I hit the ground and glanced up, the column of flame was passing right through the spot where we'd just been. Walsh, indomitable, stood his ground. The fire passed all around him without harming a hair on his head. That was one good thing about being a dragon—it made you very resistant to fire. Sadly he'd taken that ability from me.

His clothes weren't so lucky, though. Smoke rising from him where his clothes had been eaten away, Walsh stalked forward, murder in his eyes. He raised his hand to perform some surely devastating magical attack, but the eyeless witch with the wand merely cackled, twitched her wand again, and a portal opened at his feet.

He fell through without a sound, vanishing from sight, and the portal closed up behind him.

I stared at the floor where the portal had been, then to the witch, then to Ruby. Her eyes were wide.

"Whoa," she said. "That's some mojo."

"Indeed," said the witch. "Now the rest of you stand aside. That trap will hold your friend for awhile, but I'd rather not be here when he returns."

That was something, at least. If it was a trap that he could return from, that meant she wouldn't want to open it again lest he emerge. So the rest of us were probably safe from similar tricks.

But these hags had more than one trick up their sleeves, obviously.

The air stank like smoke, and one wall was blackened. I coughed as I picked myself up off the floor, and Davril did the same, drawing his blazing sword. Ruby raised her own wand.

"We're not going anywhere," she told the witches.

The one holding Gavin flicked her own wrist, cutting Gavin with the knife, and a line of blood trickled down his pale throat to stain his natty threads. He gasped in pain.

"Then your friend dies," she said.

"N-nonsense," Gavin said. "You need me to open the doors for you. You can't kill me."

"We don't need anyone. If you don't open the doors, Mistress Angela will. Her whole army will pour in and we will take this wardrobe by force."

"My fellow knights will attack," Davril said.

"Yesss," she hissed, but she spoke to Gavin, not Davril. "There will be fighting, right here in your home. War! Is that what you want? And we will get the wardrobe anyway. But work with us, allow us passage, and you will survive."

"This is such bullshit," I said.

"Silence!" she shrieked, then jerked Gavin back and forth like a rag doll. "What say you? Will you open the doors or no?"

"Don't do it," Davril said. "Their kind cannot be allowed to possess the wardrobe."

Gavin swallowed, his Adam's apple bobbing against the blade. Sweat beaded his brow and matted his hair.

"Stay strong, Gav," I said. "We've got this."

The witch with the wand flicked her hand again. It was as if a huge wind lifted me up and hurled be against the wall. I struck it with terrific force, then slid down it to crumple at the bottom.

"Jade!" Ruby cried.

Every bone in my body hurt. Groaning, I tried to rise but couldn't. Davril crouched next to me and helped me stand. Raggedly, I nodded to him, letting him know I was okay, and stood on my own. I didn't feel okay, though. But I wanted him free.

"We can destroy you all—" started the wand witch, but she didn't finish. Enraged by what had happened to me, Ruby fired a pulse of red energy at her out of her wand. The energy flashed straight toward the witch. But like before, a transparent shield shimmered into existence, and the red pulse rebounded, shooting straight for Ruby. She screamed and hit the ground, rolling. When she came to a stop, she aimed her wand at the witch again, but the witch was ready. With another flick of her hand, she fired a green blast at Ruby. There was no way Ruby could evade it in time. Fear and terror welled up inside me.

Davril lunged forward and intercepted the blast with his blade. The green pulse bounced off it, deflected toward the ceiling, where it exploded in green light. Green smoke filled the air to compete with the black.

The eyeless witch aimed the wand at Davril, incensed that he would thwart her. I gathered my strength, ripped out my crossbow and aimed it at her heart, not that she had one. Even as I fired, the crossbow exploded in my hands, hurling me backwards. I hit the wall again, but not as hard this time.

"Enough!" shouted the wand witch. She stabbed her wand at me, and a pink sticky web burst from the end of it and flew toward me, expanding as it went. It struck me, pinning me to the wall. She fired one at Davril, too, even as he was rising from the floor. It pinned him there.

Ruby was aiming her own wand as the pink web hit her, but the impact threw her aim off and a blast of freezing ice hit a lamp instead of the witch. Ruby was stuck just like the rest of us.

The other witch shook Gavin again. "Well, Minister? Will you open the door or not?"

He sighed, watching the three of us struggle futilely. "Fine. I'll do it. Just don't cause any more violence in my home."

"Excellent."

The wand witch waved her instrument and the wardrobe floated off the ground, as weightless as a feather.

I cursed at Gavin as they dragged him away, but he didn't bother to meet my eyes, and then he was gone. The wand witch towed the wardrobe behind them by magical means as they went. I heard some shouts and the sounds of fighting. Gavin's cohorts in the Guild must be coming to his rescue. For a moment hope rose in me, but then I heard screams. They weren't coming from the witches. Shortly the sounds faded, and I knew all resistance had collapsed.

I struggled, ripping at the green webbing that bound me, but it was stuck fast, and thick as concrete. Worse, it exuded a heady smell ...

My vision dimmed, blurring to almost nothing. My strength ebbed, and I started to pass out. My shifter strength flared to life, giving me the vitality enough to ward it off. Blinking, I resumed tearing at the webbing with new zeal. I didn't know how long I could resist its fumes.

Davril, meanwhile, sawed at the webbing with his sword. He let out a triumphant exclamation and tore away a long strand. Then another and another. In moments he had jumped to his feet and was approaching me.

"Stay still," he said, and slashed a long ribbon of webbing to my right. A couple of more slashes and I toppled forward.

He caught me. Panting, we stared into each other's faces.

"Ruby," I said.

I went to her. Without shifter abilities or the innate power of the Fae, the webbing had put her to sleep. Davril freed her of it and I dragged her away from it, but she was out cold.

"How long do you think before she wakes up?" I said.

"I don't know."

"But she's okay?"

"I think so. Yes, she's fine. But if we don't hurry, Angela will have that wardrobe, and with it direct access to the Shadow."

"I still don't know how that benefits her."

"Neither do I, but it obviously does. Come."

Holding his sword out before him, he jogged away, leaving the room and heading in the direction of the main doors, where Angela's army was massing. He spoke into his enchanted wristwatch as he went—summoning his own army, no doubt. The Fae Knights were going to war.

I spared Ruby one last look, then darted after him.

"Calling in the cavalry?" I asked.

"Well, the entire force, but yes, the cavalry, too. They should be ushering passers-by away from the area and setting into Angela's minions at any moment. Hopefully that will stop her if we fail."

We ran through dark halls, passing down a long staircase and through broad corridors. At last the huge main doors came in sight ahead. Sure enough, I could already hear the sounds of fighting outside—shouts and the ring of steel on steel. The two eyeless witches were approaching the doors, one still holding Gavin, the other towing the wardrobe where it floated above the ground.

"Open them now!" the first witch said.

"Very well," Gavin muttered. He said a string of words and the Guild House doors flew open.

Outside Fae Knights in armor battled the bikers, mages and bird-people that composed Angela's army. No doubt she was out there as well, leading the fight against the Fae. Was she even now glancing toward the open doors, seeing her chance?

A thunderclap shook the foyer, and I gasped at the sound and the accompanying light. There was a huge flash, and suddenly a figure stood on the threshold of the Guild House. When my eyes adjusted, I saw that it wasn't Angela.

It was Nevos.

"Hello, brother," he said.

Chapter 21

"You!" snarled Davril. He and I had just been coming on the witches from the rear, meaning to ambush them, but now they whirled, seeing us. *Thanks, Nevos.*

"You will not have the wardrobe," one hissed at us, but I was already moving. She'd let herself become distracted, allowing me to get in close.

I smashed a fist across her jaw, and she went flying, just like she'd sent me minutes ago. She didn't go so far as to hit the wall since the walls were further apart here, but she went a good ten feet, then slammed into the floor and slid along it, for the moment unconscious.

Without her to suspend it off the ground, the wardrobe fell, crashing heavily to the tiles. I hoped it would break, but its magic was too strong. It did land with a bang, though.

Enraged, the remaining witch flung Gavin at me, and while I was dodging him she whipped out her wand.

A fireball gathered on the tip and flew straight at me. Davril intercepted it with his sword. It caromed around the ceiling, finally exploding the chandelier hanging over the marble floor. The chandelier's remains fell, flaming and glittering, to the floor, and we all threw ourselves aside. Its shrapnel erupted in all directions, and I winced as something sliced my arm.

When I glanced up, the witch was stalking toward me, nursing one leg, which was bleeding. It didn't seem to have slowed her wrath any, though. Another fireball gathered on the tip of her wand.

Behind her, Nevos was doing something with the wardrobe. He was holding up a strange glass cube in the palm of one hand and casting a spell. The cube flickered, and so did the wardrobe.

My attention stayed on the witch. She advanced on me, murder in her eyes, then coiled her hand to throw the fireball. Davril was nowhere in sight. I rolled to the side. The fireball hit the marble where I'd just been. *Boom!*

I bounded to my feet, one hand holding a pile of dust and shrapnel. I hurled it at her face. She coughed and wheezed. The new fireball that had been building on the tip of her wand fizzled out.

I punched her in the belly, then across the jaw. She sagged to the floor like a sack of ugly spuds, out of the fight.

Coughing, Davril rose from the floor, picking shards of glass out of one arm. I went to him and brushed some more jagged splinters off him.

"You okay?" I said.

He nodded. He'd dropped his sword, but he scooped it up, and we both rounded on Nevos together. The wardrobe was shimmering out of existence. No, that wasn't quite right. It was disappearing from the floor but reappearing in his little glass cube, but in miniature. He'd found a way to make the huge gothic monstrosity mobile. Clever Nevos. Even as we moved toward him, the wardrobe completely vanished from the floor, now appearing very solid inside the cube, which fit on the palm of his hand.

Smiling, Nevos hung it from a clip on his waist.

"You're not going anywhere with that," Davril said.

Nevos reached to the scabbard on the other side of his waist and drew a sword, dark and gleaming, inset with jewels glimmering with strange energy.

"You can't stop me, brother," he said, fairly spitting the word.

Behind him, battle still raged in the streets, but at the moment it wasn't coming any closer. The knights and the thugs had quite enough to contend with by themselves. We probably didn't have long, though.

"I can, and I will," Davril said. "But because you are my brother, I give you this one chance. Surrender and you will not be harmed."

Nevos laughed. "I wish I could make you the same offer, but it would be a lie."

He sprang forward and hacked at Davril's head. Davril blocked the blow with a clang. His sword flashed with the impact. Bunching his shoulders, he flung Nevos back, then aimed a swipe at his abdomen. Nevos swayed backward, avoiding the blow. Sweat flew from his long black hair.

My heart pounded. My belly fluttered. The truth was I didn't want either one to die. But that might mean neither one would prevail, either. And *someone* had to win.

It had all come down to this. Brother against brother for the fate of the world.

Nevos lunged forward with a flurry of quick strikes aimed at Davril's torso. Davril's sword licked out, knocking blow after blow aside. Nevos drove him backward, jaw set, eyes hard. At last Davril found a break in the net of steel and sent a fist at Nevos's face. The fist connected and Nevos reeled back, blood trickling down his cheek.

Grimly, the two brothers circled each other.

"Screw this," I said. I stepped forward to attack Nevos.

"Don't," he said. "You're on the wrong side of this, Jade. But you don't have to be."

"Bullshit," I said. "You serve the Dark Lord!"

"Yes, and his will shall triumph. As it should. The Fae have had their chance, and they've proven themselves unworthy." He sliced at Davril's head. Davril parried. "*Davril* proved himself unworthy."

"Traitor," Davril said. "Villain. I can't believe we once played together in the yard."

Circle, circle.

"Yes, and I can't believe you betrayed me. That you seduced my wife."

Davril glared. "She and I had been promised each other since we were children! We *loved* each other."

"So you don't deny it! Good!" Nevos hacked at Davril's ankle, meaning to hobble him. Davril danced back and thrust at Nevos's unprotected throat. Nevos pirouetted gracefully, avoiding the strike, and the two resumed circling each other. "See?" Nevos said to me. "He doesn't even deny betraying me. He brought this all about, Jade. Davril, not me. He's the cause of the war. Of everything."

Tears burned my eyes. "Davril, is that true?"

Davril didn't spare me a glance, but something strange passed over his face, something like guilt. "Yes, Jade. It's true. I won't explain myself. I won't beg for forgiveness."

Nevos spat a gob of blood. "Pride! You always were a proud one, you ass."

He lunged forward, slicing at Davril's arm. Davril blocked the blow, then delivered what would have been a devastating strike at Nevos's head. Sweat flying, Nevos sprang aside, then slashed at Davril's face. Davril parried.

They were evenly matched, I saw. Neither one could best the other, or if they did it would be luck that decided the outcome.

I could make the difference. Anger burned in me, though, and hurt. Davril truly had seduced Nevos's wife and brought all this about, and he was the one who had presumed to lecture *me* on morality! The gall!

"Jade!" Nevos said. "Decide! Me or him!"

With a wild cry, I sprang. I had made my choice. The outcome was never in doubt, really. I flew through the air, a scream on my lips, and landed on my target's back. Nevos cursed beneath me, but my weight did the trick. He stumbled and tripped over a rod of the fallen chandelier. Davril rushed in and kicked him in the solar plexus. Nevos grunted and fell to his knees. I jumped off, ripped his sword loose and danced back.

Breathing heavily, Davril nodded at me. "Thank you."

"Sure."

Kneeling, Nevos glared up at us. "You think you've won, but you've won nothing." He studied me. "Jade, did you not wonder how I found you? How I knew where the wardrobe was being kept?"

"I assumed you just followed the sounds of fighting."

He shook his head. There was victory but also sadness in his eyes. "No. I used one of the oldest spells of all. I simply followed one of my hairs that was not attached to my body."

I went cold inside. Awkwardly, I looked at Davril, then back to Nevos.

"You … a hair?" Unable to stop myself, I lifted my free hand to my own hair and raked my fingers through it, as if expecting to find Nevos's missing strand there. Maybe I did, too. All I saw were a few loose dark hairs.

Nevos grunted. "You two deserve each other. Both cheaters and liars."

Davril looked stung. "Jade … Did you … *and Nevos* … ?"

Before I could answer, the tide of war finally reached us. A gaggle of knights, mages and thugs, Angela among them, spilled into the foyer from the street. Battle raged all around, everyone fighting everyone. Davril and I found ourselves fighting back to back. We did it awkwardly, though, and there was some seriously thick tension between us. When we had space to breathe, we looked for Nevos, but he, and the wardrobe he still carried, were gone.

Almost.

"There!" Davril said. He pointed to a figure cutting his way through the battle, heading outside.

"After him!" I said.

Together we ran through the battle, having to hack our way through it, and at last poured outside. Nevos's pterodactyl-like mount, the taron, was just setting down on the city street. He climbed aboard the saddle and said, "Ra!"

The taron pumped its wings and lifted off, taking to the skies. A few bikers fired guns at it, but the bullets hit a magical shield that shimmered with orange lights around the creature and were incinerated. In moments the flier and its rider had reached the height of the tallest skyscrapers. That thing could really move.

Davril whistled. Lady Kay on her gorgeous white wings rippled into visibility overhead, then settled toward the ground. Davril leapt into the driver's seat and I hauled myself into the passenger's. As he took the wheels and guided her upward, I whistled, too. Chromecat appeared, black wings pumping, and trailed close behind us.

"Go, girl!" Davril said, and stomped the gas.

Lady Kay shot forward through the canyon of steel and concrete, aimed straight at Nevos on his taron.

Nevos had obtained one of the blunderbuss-type pistols his former associate Lyra had sported, and he turned in his saddle and fired a blast at us. The gooey ball of green death sped straight at us. Davril jerked the wheel, bringing Lady Kay to the side, and the whizzing goo hurled harmlessly past.

"Do you have any guns?" I said. "I lost my crossbow."

"Sorry, no guns."

"Damn." I shook my head. "Just get me close enough. I'll jump on him. Steal the cube."

"That energy shield will fry you."

"Let me worry about that. I can disarm any shield." So I hoped, anyway.

He glanced at me sideways. "Thanks for taking my side, back there."

"You didn't make it easy for me. You could've given me a reason, you know."

"Like saving the world?"

I rolled my eyes. "Sometimes a person needs a little incentive to do the right thing. I know you have some reason why you did what you did. Did Nevos beat her? Was he cruel? Were you her protector?"

He sighed. "No. Nevos was not abusive."

"But …"

"But that will have to wait for another time."

Nevos was fast, but Lady Kay was proving faster. We were gradually gaining on the taron. I pulled my legs beneath me on the seat and crouched, ready to leap onto the hood of the car and then onto the taron. I'd have to remember to disarm the shield first and somehow not fall off the hood while I was doing it. Damn, but I really needed to look into getting a desk job.

Nevos swerved around the side of a building, and we followed. I held on tight to the door and dashboard, then looked up to get a fix on Nevos …

… and saw Walsh, huge and red and winged, in his dragon form, barreling down the canyon of steel straight at us. Or rather at Nevos. The traitorous Fae, however, hauled on the reins of his steed, bringing it up. He just barely managed to gain enough altitude to avoid Walsh's snapping jaws. The great dragon slammed his teeth shut on the empty air where Nevos had been a split second before.

Unable to follow Nevos quite as nimbly, and with us dead in his sights, Walsh drove right toward me and Davril.

"Shit!" I said.

Davril spun the wheel, hard, throwing us down a side-corridor. Behind us Walsh passed in a rage, smoke issuing from his maw.

Breathless, I glanced to Davril. "I guess the witches' holding spell couldn't hold him for long."

"Apparently not," he said. His face was sheened with sweat.

He made another turn, then another. I saw Walsh pass between two buildings, then vanish. I hoped he was going after Nevos. After all, Nevos had the wardrobe. Just as I was thinking this, Nevos himself appeared, flying his taron directly above us.

"Enjoy!" he said.

He'd tilted his mount sideways so that he could do what he did next: he flung his arm and a ball of rippling pale green magic fluttered down to us, then engulfed Lady Kay. Instantly it dispersed. Then Nevos was gone, laughing.

"What did he do?" I said.

Walsh appeared between the buildings ahead. Flame building at the back of his mouth, he saw us and barreled straight for us.

"Why isn't he going for Nevos?" I said.

Davril muttered some Fae-ish swear. "That bastard! He transferred the wardrobe's magical signature to us."

"He *what?*"

"Now Walsh thinks *we* have the wardrobe."

"That bastard!" I'd picked the right brother, all right.

"It will only last a few minutes, but that's all he needs."

Walsh gathered the fire in his maw, preparing to unleash it. Davril and I would be roasted alive. All of a sudden, a blaze of lightning forked down from the heavens and speared Walsh in the scaled back. He bellowed in pain. The fire disappeared.

Wide-eyed, I glanced behind us. Grinning, her red hair streaming behind her, Ruby raced toward us on her broom.

"Sis!" I said.

"Jade!"

She came alongside us and flicked us a thumbs up. "I woke up with a huge headache and you two nowhere in sight. I figured you must be in the shit without me."

"Language, Rubes!"

Davril was more to the point. "Can you use that lightning spell again?"

"Sadly, no. That took most of my mojo."

We turned a corner, our craft forming a tight formation, with Chromecat still flying immediately behind. I couldn't see Walsh, but I knew he must be somewhere behind the buildings I could see, and though he couldn't see us he *could* sense the wardrobe, or at least its false signature. No way we could lose him. We had to deal with him somehow.

"You have any magic that could help?" I asked Ruby.

She frowned, then patted a satchel on her saddle. "All I can think of is my anti-shifter serum."

"Your what?"

"A syringe full of a special serum. It will revert any shifter from its animal form to its human form. Pretty expensive spellgredients."

"Jeez, well I wouldn't want you to *spend* anything."

"Okay, fine, you can use it, but I don't know how you'll get it into his bloodstream. His scales are too thick." She rummaged through the satchel with the hand not guiding the broom, pulled out a capped syringe and tossed it across to me. I blinked at it, grimaced, and thrust it through my waistband.

"Don't do anything foolish," Davril said. I rejoiced at the genuine fear I heard in his voice.

"You see any non-foolish options on the table?" I asked.

He said nothing.

I'd been gathering myself to scramble forward onto the hood, but now I scrambled backward, over the back seat and onto the gleaming silver trunk of Lady Kay. I whistled. Chromecat shot forward, and I jumped into her seat. I thrilled at the feel of her engine under me, but I forced myself not to look down. It was a long way to the city streets, and I couldn't fly like I used to. Thanks to the fucker that was even then hunting us.

I joined Ruby and together we flew beside Davril in Lady Kay.

"This is crazy," Ruby said.

"You think this is crazy," I said. "Watch what happens next."

Walsh reappeared behind us, smoke trailing from his maw. "Surrender the wardrobe!" he thundered. "Surrender it or die!"

He pumped his wings and darted forward, faster than we were. Fire shot from his mouth, right toward us.

"Split up!" Davril said. "I'll draw him away!"

He twisted the wheel and shot down a side-corridor. Ruby and I veered the other way, going opposite him. The column of fire billowed harmlessly past. I turned my head to see Walsh banking with shocking nimbleness to pursue Davril. Of course. Nevos's spell had been cast on Lady Kay herself.

"Be swift," I told Davril.

I pulled Chromecat around and raced at Walsh's back. Ruby came right behind, a frightened look on her face.

Davril turned down one canyon, then another. Damn! The water was right ahead. He was going to fly out over the harbor, where there was no cover from buildings. I had to hurry. I gunned Chromecat and approached Walsh from behind. His tail whipped from side to side, almost striking me. I gasped. The tail whizzed past.

Hauling Chromecat higher, I pulled just above Walsh. His broad, scaly back was right below me. Was I really going to go through with this? Ruby was right. It was crazy.

"Screw it," I said.

I jumped from Chromecat's saddle and landed on Walsh's back near his spine. Without Chromecat's or Lady Kay's spells to protect me, the high winds whipped at me, almost hurling me over the side. I hunkered low and threw myself on my hands and knees. The heat of Walsh's scales burned my hands.

"Damn damn dam," I said, shuffling forward.

Ahead Davril had passed the last buildings of Manhattan and had shot out over open water. I could feel by the heat in Walsh's scales that the dragon was gearing up for another blast of fire. What would probably be the end of Davril.

I wasn't going to let that happen. Whatever he'd done or not done, I knew that I cared for him. He wasn't going to die on my watch.

I scrabbled out onto Walsh's neck, going faster now.

"Now you die!" Walsh roared at Davril, and prepared to roast Lady Kay.

"I don't think so," I said. Reaching his head, I yanked out the syringe, ripped off the cap and plunged the needle into Walsh's right eye. He screamed. I pushed the plunger. The fire died in his maw.

"What have you done?" he said.

"You took my wings, now I'm taking yours."

Ruby's concoction worked immediately. Walsh's neck shrank and his scales disappeared, replaced by human skin. In seconds he was simply a human man falling toward the ocean. And me beside him. I whistled and Chromecat appeared below me. I fell into the saddle hard, then veered her to the side.

Walsh didn't scream as he fell. He plummeted, scowling and wrathful, and I had no doubt I would see him again.

He struck the sea and vanished from sight. Breathless, I watched the white mark on the ocean where'd he gone, but I saw no further sign of him.

Ruby came to hover beside me, then Davril.

"He'll be back," Davril said, his voice grim.

"He'd better be," I said. "He still has my fire."

"Think Nevos is still catchable?" Ruby said.

We fanned out, searching for him, but Nevos, and the wardrobe, were gone. If nothing else, at least the fighting around the Guild House had died down. When we returned there, the Lord Commander of the Order of the Shield was assisting Gavin in cleaning up. Angela and her army were gone. Once they'd realized the wardrobe was no longer present, they'd slipped away back to Shadowpark.

"I wonder if Nevos will make good on his threat," I said.

"What do you mean?" Ruby asked.

We were watching Davril confer with Lord Gleamstone. Jessela was nearby and we waved at each other.

"He said that once he had the wardrobe, there were many in Angela's camp that would follow him. That he would become their leader. I guess maybe he thinks of himself as some sort of high priest to the Shadow."

Ruby made a face. "That sounds ominous."

"Well, he is the only one on this plane, at least that I know of, that can commune openly with Lord Vorkoth now."

"Again, you're not encouraging me."

I smiled and hugged her. "But at least I have you. We couldn't have survived the day without my little sister."

She hugged back, then pulled away, studying me. "What's wrong? I know Nevos got what he wanted, but at least we're still here, right?"

But what I heard was *We're still hair.*

I ran my fingers through my black-and-purple waves, then analyzed them, still searching for Nevos's lost specimen.

Nothing.

But it was there, somewhere. And Davril knew it.

Jade, what have you done?

EPILOGUE

"Well, it's not there," Davril said. Master of the obvious.

"Yeah. Thanks for the heads up."

Together we sat in Lady Kay, staring out at the empty sky. It was where Vincent Walsh's zeppelin, his aerial mansion, had been just a couple of days ago, but it was no longer in the same place. Of course. The bastard had probably pulled up stakes as soon as he'd dragged himself out of the water.

"We should have come here first thing," I said.

"Well, we did have some cleanup to do downtown."

That was true enough. The battle had been yesterday, and the city authorities had not been pleased with the Fae Lords over what had gone down. It was the second major battle involving them in a matter of months, and though the last one had happened in a deserted stadium, this one had been all too public. Fortunately no civilians had gotten hurt.

"There goes my chance at getting my fire back," I said. I wanted to throw my feet up on the dash in protest at what the fates had bestowed upon me, but I knew Davril hated that, and Lady Kay probably wasn't a big fan, either.

"I'm sorry, Jade. There will be other chances. At least we know what his zeppelin looks like now. We'll be watching for it."

"Yeah, and I'm sure he won't try to disguise it at all."

Then again, fair was fair. Ruby and I had to switch apartments now that Walsh knew where we lived. It served him right to have to relocate, too, and I was petty enough to enjoy the thought of his aggravation. Then again, simply parking his zeppelin in a different spot and casting a spell on it to change its appearance wasn't much of a bother for the likes of him.

But I would give him some bother, all right. Real soon. *You'd best be looking over your shoulder, Vinnie.*

"Well, shall we go back to the Palace?" Davril said.

"I guess."

The Queen had given us a day off after all the action, and Davril had been kind enough to take me here even though we both knew what the likely outcome was going to be. We'd been prepared to call in the army, though. Not just for my fire, but to capture an enemy of the Fae.

As Davril turned the wheel and brought Lady Kay around, I said, "Interesting that he seems to hate the Shadow. All he did, it was to stop someone from being able to commune with Lord Vorkoth."

Davril nodded. "There's more to Walsh than we understand, that's for certain. We don't know what his real agenda is."

We drove along. Clouds scudded around us. Lady Kay's white wings pumped slowly to either side, lovingly stroking the air. I loved how the sunlight bounced off them. Slowly, very slowly, I turned to Davril.

"So," I said.

He didn't reply, just stared forward.

"So. Are you finally going to tell me? What really did happen between you and Nevos?"

For a long moment, he said nothing. Then he let out a long breath and nodded again, this time to himself, as if trying to convince him of something.

"I suppose you've earned the truth," he said. "You trusted me in the moment of crisis without demanding an explanation."

"Well, gah, thanks, Mr. Roboto. So spill!"

"Jade, patience."

I forced myself to settle back down. In a calmer tone of voice, I said, "Please. Tell me. If you would."

The city was far below us, and the sky was very blue around us as he began:

"It started long, long ago to your way of looking at things. Over two hundred years ago, when I was young, and so was Liana. Nevos wasn't much older. Well, Liana was the daughter of a lord sworn to my father's service, and we played together a great deal, and were inseparable. In appreciation of that, my father and her father agreed that we would be promised to each other, that we would wed when we were old enough, if we both agreed." Surprisingly, he smiled, and there was something boyish and wistful about it that recalled the young man he must once have been. He was still young in body, but he was hardened and cynical now. But back then he must have been truly boyish and optimistic.

"Liana and I had entered our teens, and we were very much in love," he continued. "We couldn't wait for our wedding day. I would be the prince and she my princess. Nevos would be king when Father passed, which we all hoped would be long years away. But even Fae age, and Father had had us when he was very old. He was already beginning to fade, and he began taking a great interest in making sure Nevos, the firstborn, would be ready to lead.

"I knew that Nevos was a cad and a scoundrel. He would rather go out drinking and carousing than attend to his studies or his martial training. I did all those things because I wanted to learn and better myself without any expectation of sitting the throne. Well, it so happened that

Nevos was in love with Liana. I had suspected, but it quickly became evident when he would fly into rages after he saw us together. Once he even accosted me, and I was forced to defend myself, leaving him with a black eye. This further sent Nevos into his downward spiral, and he drank more and fought more, bullying servants under him and assaulting the townspeople when in his cups.

"Eventually Father said enough was enough. Nevos was not fit to rule after he was gone. Though it pained Father greatly, he removed his blessing from Nevos and placed it on me. He made me his heir."

I shook my head. "That must have gone over well."

One corner of Davril's mouth twisted up in wry amusement. But then sadness touched his eyes. "In your terms, Nevos went ballistic. He overturned tables and chairs, defaced paintings. He took his friends out hunting in the woods for days on end, and they would return drunken and dirty. Some said they raided the towns of other provinces. Some say they had found a band of goblin raiders and begun consorting with them, perhaps even selling them captured humans for use as slaves."

"Damn!"

Davril's hands tightened on the wheel. "Father went to him. He asked Nevos what he could do to make it up to him, to put Nevos at peace again. Or at least to stop causing chaos. Nevos, of course, said he wanted the throne. Father refused. Then Nevos said the thing that would change my life, and all of our lives."

I could guess that part. "He said he wanted Liana."

Breath hissed out between Davril's teeth, but there was relief on his face, too. He was glad that I was getting it.

"To Father's shame, he said yes. He told Nevos that he would allow Liana to wed him instead of me, if she was agreeable, and if that would settle Nevos down and cause him to be an upright prince again. Liana wept and agonized over the decision, but in the end she believed it was best for the kingdom. Even though it meant the end of our happiness, she agreed to the betrothal."

"I'm so sorry."

He blinked, and I wasn't sure if it was my imagination or not but I would have sworn that there was moisture in his eyes. "It was .... a difficult time," he admitted.

Wind whispered over the hood of Lady Kay. Only some of it seeped through the magical barriers, just enough to ruffle my hair, but I barely felt it. I was far away, in that other land, side by side with a young, tormented Davril Stormguard. I pictured him gazing out of a castle tower, staring across the gulf at another tower, where Nevos made love to his new bride and Davril balled his fists in rage.

"What happened?" I said after some time.

"Nevos did indeed settle down, at least somewhat. Father died, and I became king. Nevos, though more princely, still went out drinking and sleeping with any woman he wanted to. Rumors spread of his deeds, and Liana was embarrassed before the entire kingdom. She was shamed. Weeping, she came to me. If nothing else, we had been friends since childhood, and she could confide in me. But something happened. She was vulnerable, and I suppose I was, too. We loved each other, yet had never ..."

I gasped. "You were saving yourselves for marriage."

He sighed. "So it was."

I chewed on my lower lip. "So you slept together."

"To our shame, yes. Passion overcame us. This happened again and again over several months, before at last Nevos caught us. Enraged, he rushed at me. Tried to kill me. I just barely fended him off. I wounded him with a slash across his side. He retreated to his tower and gathered his supporters. He had been grooming his own men, most of them criminals and miscreants. Men who were attracted to dark deeds and willing to follow someone who promised them the ability to fulfill their most depraved fantasies. Knowing that he wanted a coup, I summoned my own troops.

"Civil war loomed, and it looked like the kingdom would be ripped apart. Liana couldn't bear knowing that she had caused this. She went to Nevos, or tried to, in an effort to talk him down from violence. One of his men was jumpy, though, and thought she was an enemy. He killed her."

"My God!"

"After that, we saw weird lights in Nevos's tower and heard rumor of strange sorceries. I know now that he must have reached out to the dark powers, perhaps through the goblins he had met earlier. He found a way to commune with Lord Vorkoth, to make common cause with him. He opened the gates of the castle and the city to the hordes of the Shadow, starting the Great War, and you know the rest."

"I'm so sorry, Davril. That's terrible."

He brought Lady Kay lower and threaded her between the spires of Manhattan. Fantastic castles and palaces sprouted from the tallest towers, sunlight winking on the facets of their windows. Ahead reared the glory of the Great Palace itself. Home of the Fae Queen. My home, too, at least part of the time.

Davril brought Lady Kay into the hangar and let the stablemaster take over. Silent and pensive, we walked through the halls back to the tower where the Order of the Shield operated out of. A heaviness settled on me, and a huge sadness. I grieved for Liana and the Davril that was, for the happiness that could have been.

Davril escorted me to my room. Still silent, thinking, I let him open the door for me.

"So," he said at last. "Do you still doubt me?"

Tears burned my eyes. "God, no." I reached out and touched his arm, then hastily withdrew my hand.

He met my gaze, then dropped his own. In a low voice, he said, "*I* do. I'm the cause of all this, Jade. My actions led us to this point. And now Nevos has found a new way to commune with his Master. Dire things happened last time that happened."

"We won't allow that to happen again."

I wanted to kiss him, but I could tell from the reserve in his face that that would be a bad idea. Maybe a very bad idea.

He raised his eyes, and a new note had entered his face. I thought I knew that expression, but I wasn't sure. Not until he lifted a hand and ran it through my hair, then glanced at his fingers afterward.

Shame and guilt tore at me, and I wanted to crawl in a hole and vanish from the world.

"I ..."

"Yes?" he said.

I swallowed. "I'm ... sorry. I mean, I only did it to get the knob. I mean ... you know what I mean."

"And you couldn't have simply struck him over the head or found some other way to render him unconscious once you got him alone? You had to sleep with him?"

I opened my mouth to reply, then closed it. There was nothing to say.

Davril nodded sadly and moved off down the hall. I started to call out for him, but the words died in my throat. He was still my partner, I knew. That hadn't changed. And tomorrow we would go out and find new bad guys to take down. But how could we ever get back to the place we were before Nevos had entered our lives? Or reentered, in his case? I was the second woman Nevos had bedded ahead of his brother. That must be part of it, too. But there was more than that. There were real feelings between Davril and I.

And I'd just really screwed that up.

I closed the door, threw myself on the bed and cried. Damn it all, what was I going to do now?

THE END

46935370R00130

Made in the USA
Columbia, SC
27 December 2018